Black S

C

Sally Lovell

Black Security Company

Chance Black Book 3

Sally Lovell

Table of Contents

Chapter 1

Chance Black finished up the security system he had worked on for the last month. It had been an enormous job setting up all the cameras in the building of a financial company. Chance could only work after the employees left for the day. The owner didn't want the employees to know the cameras' locations. The owner had been particular about where each camera was placed. Chance had made some suggestions that the owner had agreed to. Once the cameras had been set up, Chance and the owner went around to fix specific cameras at different angles so the owner's satisfaction. Chance had tried to maintain his patience with the owner since the job was paying over $300,000.00, and he would have to come back to do updates when needed.

Chance was a single guy, which was good since he had been living out of a suitcase and a hotel for a few months. He had been installing security systems nonstop. Chance wasn't complaining, but he was tired. There was a lot of money selling and installing security systems. Chance and his three brothers owned Black Security Company. The business was doing great in picking up new clients and had an excellent reputation for getting any job done professionally.

Black Security had a whole load of clients that kept them very busy. Chance and his brothers were all former military. Carter, the oldest, was ex-Black Ops. Chase was an ex-Navy SEAL, Colin was an ex-Marine, and Chance was an ex-Air Force.

Chance had left the Air Force after spending four years in Afghanistan. He flew a rescue helicopter to pick up the injured soldiers. He still wore the scars from Afghanistan on his shoulder and arm from taking bullets. His helicopters had been shot down twice without him being injured and escaping before being taken captive. Chance figured he would get out while he was fully intact. Carter offered him a partnership in Black Security. Chance decided to take the offer and work with his brothers.

Carter, the oldest brother, and founder of Black Security, mainly stayed in the office now. Since his wife Lillie was pregnant with their first child. That left Chance, Chase, and Colin to do most of the security jobs. Chase would fly out every other week to see his rocker girlfriend, Jaci Hurst. Jaci was on tour for a year in the States.

Jaci was becoming more famous than ever. Jaci and Chase tried to keep their relationship on the quiet side, but Chase's face would end up in the tabloids once in a while with her. After all, Chase did save her from Mark Kennedy, who was her music manager and stalker. That had been a terrible mess with many twists and turns for Chase and Jaci, with Mark Kennedy dead.

Chance would snicker every time seeing pictures of his brother decked out in leathers. He and Colin loved to tease Chase about the leather outfits. Chase would get pissed off at them but would eventually get over it. Chase was after dating a famous rock singer with a bad girl image.

Chance and Colin were the only two singles left in the family. Which was fine. Chance was in no hurry to get married any time soon. Besides, right now, Chance had no time to date. He was not complaining but did miss dating a little bit. It had been at least six months since he had been with a woman.

The last relationship Chance was in lasted a year with the same woman. Chance had thought she was possibly the one he would marry. But after six months, her true colors started showing. The woman, Kristy, would get pissed off when he would leave for a month at a time for work. She couldn't understand why the company didn't hire other people to do the "grunge work," as she would say. Chance tried to make her understand numerous times that was not how he and his brothers worked. They all put time and effort into making it a profitable and respectable business.

Kristy decided she couldn't trust him when he worked in a different state or city, believing he was fooling around with other women when he was away from her. Chance got tired of her accusations, breaking things off with Kristy.

Chance smiled as he walked into his house after being away for several months. He threw his suitcase on the floor and flopped down on his bed.

"Damn, I missed you," Chance smiled, telling this to his bed. He sat up, grabbed his suitcase off the floor, and took it into the laundry room. He tossed his dirty clothes into the washing machine. His phone vibrated in his pocket. Chance pulled the cell phone out of his pocket and laughed.

"Hello," Chance said, smiling.

"Hey, Chance, how's it going?" Justin Beard asked.

"Justin, I just walked through the door. I have been on the road for a couple months installing security systems."

"No shit. Well, Dean and I are in your neck of the woods tonight. We have a couple days left from our leave before heading back to the base. We were wondering if you wanted to meet us down at Heller's Honky Tonk Bar?"

"Sure, I have nothing going on except laundry."

"What the fuck, laundry? You are getting too domesticated now that you are no longer in the Air Force. Next, you will be telling us you're getting married and having babies."

"Um, that is not happening for a little while yet."

"Where is that, Kathy, or Kris or whatever the hell her name is that you were dating for the last year?"

"Split up. I have been single for the last six months. I don't have the time to date right now. We are super busy at the security business."

"Hey, I have seen your brother Chase in the tabloids with rock singer Jaci Hurst here and there. Is he doing security for her?"

"Yes and no, Chase is actually dating Jaci Hurst. I will have to give you the whole story tonight."

"No shit, he is dating a famous rock singer. That is fucking great. I can't wait to hear this. Okay, so we will see you tonight."

"I will be there later, Justin." Chance hung up his phone, smiling.

Chance had been in the Air Force with Justin Beard and Dean Soul. They all had signed up at the same time. The three of them ended up being best friends and comrades. They were sent over to Afghanistan together. Justin had been Chance's co-pilot. Justin and Dean were still serving in the Air Force.

When he decided to leave, Chance served twelve years in the Air Force. After spending eight years of the twelve in Afghanistan and being shot down a couple of times, and receiving two bullet holes in his body, Chance had been ready to get out. Chance loved being a pilot in the Air Force, but eight years of a war going nowhere took its toll on him. Chance still flies every chance he gets and keeps his pilot license current.

So, when his brother Carter offered him a piece of ownership of Black Security, Chance jumped on it. Chance and his three brothers work great together. They all knew what had to be done and got it done to the best of their ability.

Chapter 2

Nikki Curtis had thought she would make a career in the Air Force, but it didn't turn out as she had hoped. A woman in the armed forces had to have pretty thick skin to take the other guys' ribbing, but eventually, she grew tired of it.

Justin Beard and Dean Morris befriended her right away in the Air Force. They stayed close friends even after she got out. They had always bragged about their third friend Chance Black. The three guys had been very tight and served together for twelve years until Chance Black left the Air Force. Nikki had just finished boot camp and was becoming a pilot when their friend Chance left. So, Nikki had never met the famous Chance Black. She just heard a lot about him from Justin and Dean.

Nikki's life had been turned upside down two years ago after leaving the Air Force. A man, Jack Collins, whom she had been dating for two years while in the Air Force, gave her a hell of a surprise. Nikki had told Jake she was thinking about possibly leaving the Air Force. Jake tried to talk her out of it, saying she would have difficulty finding a job. Nikki reminded Jake it was her decision to make. So, when she decided to leave, Nikki didn't tell Jake. Nikki chose to surprise Jake instead. That was the day her life turned inside out.

Nikki had spent a couple of days in bed with Jake a month prior. Jake had come to the base because she had a couple of days of leave to use. They had spent the entire two days in bed, only getting up to eat. The two days had been fantastic. They had talked about their future together. Jake had surprised her with an engagement ring. Nikki thought her life couldn't get any better. The only issue they had not discussed was Nikki leaving the Air Force. Jake had left, and Nikki was on cloud nine thinking about her future with Jake.

Nikki had been feeling really nauseous the last couple of weeks. She finally broke down and went to see the doctor on base, only to find out she was pregnant. Nikki wasn't sure how she felt about having a baby yet. It definitely had not been in her plans. Jake and she hadn't really talked about having kids. Nikki spoke to the doctor about her options, so she knew she had a little time to think about it but not much. Nikki wanted to see how Jake would feel about the baby before she did anything.

On her last day in the Air Force, the guys in her squad, with Justin and Dean, took her to the bar. They gave her an excellent goodbye party. She just hadn't been in the mood to party with the pregnancy weighing heavy on her mind. Justin and Dean were the only two to notice she was pretending to drink.

"Nikki, what is up with you, babe?" Justin asked.

"What do you mean?" Nikki replied.

"Babe, I know you. You haven't drank any of the shots being bought for you." Justin gave her a concerned look.

"I must drive home. So, I don't want to get hammered. I have a 24-hour drive ahead of me."

"Nikki, you have not even touched one shot. I saw you pour it into the water glass."

"Shit."

"Shit is right. What is going on with you? Did you finally send that asshole Jake packing?" Justin asked hopefully. Nikki shook her head and then held up her hand.

"Um...no. We are actually engaged, Justin."

"What! When did that fucking happen?" Justin yelled.

"A month ago, when I had a couple days of leave. Jake came here, and we spent a couple of days together."

"Nikki, you know I love you, right?" Justin said sincerely. Nikki nodded her head waiting for his comment.

"I know, Justin. You and Dean are my best friends."

"Girl, I don't like Jake. Something about him bothers me, and I can't figure it out."

"I know, so you will not like what I will say next."

"What, Nikki, am I not going to like it?" Justin asked, staring at her with uncertainty.

"I...um...I am pregnant." Nikki said softly. Justin shook his head in denial.

"Fuck, Nikki, fuck!" Justin yelled loudly enough to make Dean walk over, standing by Justin.

"What am I missing over here?" Dean asked curiously.

"Nikki just told me she is fucking pregnant," Justin stated harshly. Dean held up his hands in denial.

"Not mine," Dean said smartly.

"Not mine either. Would you like to guess who the father is?" Justin asked. Dean glanced at Nikki and then at Justin, shaking his head.

"The prick Jake," Dean replied. Justin nodded his head. "Damn, Nikki, Jake is a fucking loser."

Justin cleared his throat and pointed to Nikki's ring finger. Dean's eyes grew wide with surprise.

"Fuck, you are fucking engaged to Jake?" Dean growled. Nikki nodded her head.

"Sorry, the heart chose to love Jake," Nikki stated.

"Stupid heart. What is the head saying about carrying his child, happy or unsure?" Justin asked. Nikki chewed on her bottom lip before replying.

"Unsure," Nikki said softly.

"Why are you unsure? You are engaged, right?" Dean stated.

"Yes, but we never discussed having children," Nikki replied.

"I think that should be an important issue to discuss when engaged," Justin said.

"Yes, you are correct, but we didn't," Nikki said softly.

"Why is Jake not here to help you drive back and pack your things up?" Dean asked curiously. Nikki twisted and turned the paper napkin she was holding nervously. She took a deep breath before answering Justin and Dean.

"Jake doesn't know I am done with the Air Force," Nikki stated.

"Fuck Nikki! Jake is in for two big ass surprises."

"Yes, I know. The part about being pregnant, I will decide if it fits into my life right now before I tell Jake."

"That might be a good idea," Justin said.

"Let's change the subject. You both will come to look me up when you come to my state and city, right?" Nikki asked.

"Fuck yes. Our best friend Chance Black lives in Sugar Springs also."

"No shit, that is terrific. Maybe I can finally meet the notorious Chance Black," Nikki said, smiling.

"Maybe."

"It is getting late, and I have a long drive ahead of me. Thank you both for everything. I am going to miss you, shitheads." Nikki said, smiling. Justin grabbed hold of her, giving Nikki a tight bear hug.

"If you need anything, like kicking Jake's ass for some reason, you will call me, and I will be there," Justin stated firmly. Dean grabbed her, giving her a tight hug. He also said the same thing. Nikki quickly left the bar before Justin and Dean saw the tears fall down her cheeks.

Nikki left the following morning early and hauled ass toward home. She had a lot of time to think as she drove home. Nikki made up her mind. She was going to surprise Jake. Once she got settled at home, Nikki drove to Jake's house. Jake had no idea that Nikki knew his address. She had seen his driver's license and then memorized the address.

Jake had never told her where he lived, nor had she ever been there. Jake would come over to her apartment when Nikki was home on leave. Nikki was excited and nervous to see Jake.

Nikki found his house on Evergreen Street. She pulled up to the curb in front of his house. The house was nice white ranch style with a two-car garage. The lawn was nice and grew with a good size front yard. The landscaping was clean and neat, packed with a ray of colorful flowers and bushes.

Jake's black Silverado truck and a white Chevy car sat in the driveway. Nikki was slightly confused by the kids' toys in the front yard. A couple of bikes, balls, and a ball were lying in the yard. Nikki smiled, thinking maybe the toys belonged to Jake's brother's children. Nikki got out of her car and went to the front door. Just as she was going to knock, the door opened up. A woman with brown shoulder-length hair and blue eyes stared at her curiously.

"Can I help you?" the woman asked. Nikki looked around, a little confused, thinking she might have the wrong house.

"Um...I am looking for Jake Collins. Do I have the right place?"

"Who might you be?" the woman asked.

"Um...I am Nikki Curtis, Jake's fiancée."

"What? Did you just say, fiancée?" The woman blared out. Nikki nodded, then held her hand, showing the woman her ring. Nikki then noticed the anger and tears falling down the woman's face,

"Oh my god! Did something happen to Jake?" Nikki asked worriedly, seeing the tears falling down the woman's face. A little boy was tugging on the woman's pant legs. Nikki was so confused and scared about what was happening.

"Momma, who is the lady," the boy asked, staring at Nikki curiously.

"Teddy, go find your father," The woman managed to squeak out.

"Do I have the wrong house?" Nikki asked, confused.

"No, you have the right house," The woman said firmly.

"Okay, where is Jake?" Nikki asked, feeling nervous and awkward.

“Peggy, what the hell is going on?" Jake asked, walking to the front door. Nikki knew she was at the fight house after hearing Jake's voice. Peggy waved her hand at Nikki.

“Would you like to tell me what the fuck is going on, Jake?” Peggy asked angrily.

"What are you waving at?" Jake asked, walking to the front door. Jake's eyes widened, and he took a deep breath seeing Nikki standing at his front door.

"Nikki? What the hell are you doing here?" Jake asked nervously.

"I could ask the same question to you," Nikki replied, still confused.

"I am Peggy Collins. Jake's wife, and you said you are his fiancée, right?" Peggy asked.

"What! You are fucking married?” Nikki yelled in shock. “Oh my god!:" Nikki quickly turned and ran off the porch, feeling sick.

“Nikki, wait!” Jake yelled after her.

"Don't you fucking dare come near me, Jake," Nikki screamed, running to her car.

"Please, Nikki, let me explain," Jake yelled.

“There is nothing to explain. You are fucking married with fucking children. Stay the fuck away from me. I never ever want to lay eyes on you ever again." Nikki stated, climbing into her car. She squealed out into the road feeling like her heart had pulled out of her chest and devasted that she trusted him.

The following day, Nikki terminated the pregnancy without looking back. She moved on with her life. Nikki started her own charter business. She was currently financing a plane to fly goods for customers. She had landed a repeat customer with the Stamos family, that paid very well to fly cargo to Costa Rica. The Stamos family basically paid her lease payments a month of $50,000.00. Sometimes, she made an extra $50,000.00 if they needed it immediately. The other small deliveries she made paid her rent on her apartment and the rest of her bills. Life was good for her again.

Nikki had just finished a small delivery when her telephone rang. She grabbed her phone and answered it.

"Hey girl, what's up?" Justin said.

"Oh my god, Justin," Nikki squealed in delight.

"Hey, Dean and I are in your city. Want to come out and play?" Justin asked.

"I would love to. Where do you want to meet?"

"How about Heller's Honky Tonk Bar?"

"Sounds great. What time?"

"How about around 5:00p.m.? Will that work for you?"

"Sound great. I will see you there."

"Sure will."

Nikki hung up her phone with a huge smile on. She finished the inspection on her plane and then headed home to prepare for her outing with Justin and Dean.

Chapter 3

Chance walked into the bathroom and turned the shower on. He climbed inside, quickly washed up, and climbed back out, wrapping a towel around his waist. Chance dried off. He pulled on a pair of clean jeans. Chance grabbed a white T-shirt pulling it on over his head. He walked back into the bathroom, brushed his teeth, then finger-combed his short-cropped, dark brown hair. Chance walked out of the bathroom. He sat on the edge of the bed and pulled on his boots.

Chance entered the kitchen, grabbed his keys, and headed to the garage. He climbed into his truck, pushed the garage door opener then backed out of the garage. Chance pulled out onto the road, heading towards the bar.

About fifteen minutes later, Chance pulled into the parking lot of Heller's HonkieTonk Bar to meet up with Justin and Dean. The parking lot was full already. Chance found a parking space pulled his truck into it, then climbed out. Chance entered the bar. The place was crowded with customers, and the dance floor was busy. There was a country band playing real county music. Chance looked around for his Air Force buddies.

Chance spotted them on the left side of the bar in the far corner. Chance walked towards them and noticed a beautiful blonde woman sitting with them. He approached the table with a smile.

"There's our man," Justin, his air bubby, hollered out, waving his hand to Chance. Dean, his other friend, turned around, smiling.

"Hey, Chance, it's about time you showed up. We have already had a few beers waiting for you." Dan chuckled, holding up his beer. The beautiful woman turned her head sideways and smiled at Chance.

"I was working out of town and just got back today. Sorry if I am late." Chance laughed.

"Just sit your ass down and grab a beer," Justin said. Justin pulled a cold beer bottle out of the ice bucket in the center of the table. He handed it to Chance.

"Thank you, Justin." Chance said, opening the beer and taking a quick sip.

"Hey Chance, this is Nikki Curtis," Dean said, jester to the blonde woman at the table.

"Nice to meet you, Nikki," Chance smiled and sat in the empty chair beside her.

"Nikki was also in the Air Force. She just got out." Dean said, wiggling his eyebrows.

"Is that so? Nikki, how long were you enlisted?" Chance asked, turning his attention to her.

"Six years," Nikki replied, smiling.

Chance felt his cock jerk in his pants at Nikki's beautiful smile. Nikki's green eyes light up, looking at Chance. There seemed to be an instant attraction between them.

Nikki had short spiky blonde hair and green eyes. She had a heart-shaped face with a perky little nose. Her lips were luscious and pouty. Her dimples showed when she smiled. Chance thought she was gorgeous and sexy.

The white blouse Nikki wore molded to her large breasts showing off some nice cleavage. The short navy pencil skirt molded to her curvy hips nicely, showing off her slim-toned body. The short skirt also showcased her long, toned legs.

"Chance, here, owns Black Security Company with his brothers now that he is out of the Air Force," Justin said, smiling at Nikki. Nikki turned and smiled at Chance.

"Now that sounds like fun. I have my own plane. I fly a lot of cargo to Costa Rica." Nikki stated.

"So, you are done with the Air Force?" Chance asked curiously.

"I have been out for about three months. I bought a plane and have a small flying business." Nikki said.

Dean and Justin smiled at Chance. They could see the interest and attraction between Chance and Nikki.

"Hey, bro, two hot-looking women are up at the bar. They are giving me and Justin the come hinder looks." Dean said, smiling.

"Go for it. Don't let me stop you guys." Chance said, laughing, shaking his head in amusement.

"Cool, see you in a few," Justin said, standing up. Justin and Dean headed towards the women at the bar, leaving Chance and Nikki alone.

Nikki looked down at Chance's hands on the table to see if he had a ring mark or was wearing a wedding band. She smiled to herself, seeing neither on his finger. Maybe it was her night to finally meet someone decent.

Those two are such male whores. They are always leaving me at the bars by myself while they hook up with women," Nikki laughed.

"Well, you are not alone this time," Chance said, smiling.

"You are right. They finally left me with a hot man."

"Well, I don't know about being hot. You are the gorgeous one." Chance smiled. Nikki's cheeks flushed pink.

"Um...thank you," Nikki replied.

"Tell me about your flying business," Chance said curiously.

" I am for hire for small cargo deliveries. I deliver the client's cargo on time and make excellent money while doing it?"

"Whatever the client wants, as long as it is legal to load, and it will fit in my plane."

"So, you inspect the cargo to ensure it is legal?" Chance asked, concerned. Nikki gave him a surprised look.

"Most of the time, yes. I do if it is a new client," Nikki replied cautiously.

"I am not telling you how to run your business, but you should always inspect the cargo."

"Most of my clients are repeat customers. I have delivered for them lots of times. Mostly bolts of material and dried goods."

"Nowadays, you can't be too careful."

"Yes, that is very true in some cases."

Chance grabbed another beer out of the bucket. He opened it up and took a big swig. Nikki watched him swallow and thought he was absolutely gorgeous. Nikki couldn't believe her luck to be left with such a hot man tonight. Usually, when Dean and Justin left her, Nikki would have to fend off a few losers. For some reason, Nikki attracted assholes, not men that look like Chance Black.

Chance Black stood 6"2 with broad shoulders. He had big, muscled arms with the Air Force symbol tattooed on his bicep. Chance had short, cropped dark brown hair with blue eyes. His jaw was chiseled with a beautiful straight nose. Dimples showed on his cheek when he smiled.

Chance had a perfect v-line with slim hips and long muscled legs. His white t-shirt molded nicely to his broad chest. His jeans also molded to his ass and showed off his nice package in the front.

Nikki was definitely attracted to Chance. She wanted to bend her head over to Chance and run her tongue up and down his neck while he drank his beer. Nikki felt suddenly warm and flushed from her thoughts. Chance glanced over at Nikki catching her staring at him.

"Do I have something on my face, or did I dribble beer down my chin?" Chance teased, smiling.

"Neither. You are just pleasant to look at." Nikki replied. Chance shook his head, laughing at her bluntness.

"I am glad you like what you see because I know I do."

Nikki felt her body warm up again and flush more at his statement. Chance stared at her with a grin and winked at Nikki. Nikki moistened her lips and smiled. Chance's eyes tracked her pink tongue as it ran over her lips. He had the urge to bend over to take her tongue into his mouth to nip and suck on it.

Chance wondered if Nikki tasted as good as she looked. He felt his cock respond to his thought and push against his zipper. Chance shifted in the chair to get his cock in a more comfortable position. He definitely felt a strong attraction to this woman. It had been a while since Chance was in a relationship with a woman. He had been so busy with Black Security that it had been about a year and a half since he had a serious relationship and about six months since he had sex.

"Would you like to dance with me?" Nikki asked him softly.

"Sure, I would love to." Chance smiled, pushing his chair back and standing up.

Chance held out his hand to Nikki. Nikki glanced up at Chance, grabbed his hand, and stood up. Chance was surprised that she was only a few inches shorter than him.

Nikki started walking ahead of him. Chance put his hand on the lower part of her back as his eyes roamed over the back side of her. His eyes admired how the short navy skirt molded to her nice tight ass as it swayed back and forth ahead of him. Nikki could feel the heat from his hand touching her through the blouse at the lower part of her back, making her skin feel on fire.

Nikki quickly turned to face him once they were out on the dance floor. She smiled, wrapping her arms around his neck. Chance put his hand on her hips, then pulled her nice and close to his big body.

Their eyes locked on each other. Chance saw Nikki's face flush pink as he stared into her beautiful green eyes. Her tongue snuck out to moisten her suddenly dry lips. Their bodies began to sway and move together to the music. Nikki snuggled closer to Chance, liking the feel of his strong arms enclosing her body. Her fingers began to play with his short hair at the collar of his shirt.

Chance breathed in her sweet scent of roses as it wrapped around him. They were cheek to cheek. Chance heard Nikki humming to the music. Nikki started to move more sensually against him. Chance followed her lead. They moved as one grinding and swaying to the music. Chance felt his cock grow hard as he rubbed her pelvis against him. He could feel her hard nipples poking his chest and knew she was getting aroused. Chance enjoyed the feeling of her body moving against his.

"Damn, you are one hard man," Nikki whispered. Chance chuckled at her comment.

"I do try to stay in shape." Chance snickered.

"I like that. I do not like flabby men. I like men who are hard all over."

"Neither do I. I don't like flabby men either." Chance snickered. Nikki slapped his arm playfully.

"God, I hope you are into women. Usually, the gorgeous ones are always taken or gay."

"I do like women. I don't swing the other way, and I am presently single."

"Great to know because I usually attract losers or married men, not sexy, hot men like yourself."

"You are the one that's sexy as hell."

"Thank you," Nikki said. The song ended. Chance and Nikki pulled apart with regret. They walked hand and hand back to the table. Chance pulled the chair out for her to sit down. Nikki smiled at him.

"You are hot and a gentleman also. My night just keeps getting better and better."

"I am glad you are enjoying yourself. I know I am."

" I really am, thanks to you." Nikki sat in the chair. Chance pulled out the chair and sat next to her. Chance grabbed two more beers out of the bucket. He opened them both and handed Nikki one. Justin walked towards them with a smile on his face.

"I bet they are leaving with those two women they just met," Nikki said, laughing.

"You think so?" Chance asked.

"I know so," Nikki replied. Justin smiled at them and stood next to Chance.

"Hey, Chance, can you take Nikki home. Dean and I are leaving with the ladies. They invited us to a private party at their apartment," Justin said, wiggling his eyebrows and smiling.

"Sure, if Nikki doesn't mind me taking her home." Chance replied, glancing at Nikki. Nikki nodded her head.

"Go ahead, Justin. I am fine with Chance." Nikki stated.

"Great, sorry, Chance, we didn't catch up on things," Justin said, shaking Chance's hand.

"Next time, go have fun. I will catch up with you guys when you are in town again." Chance said, smiling. Justin punched him in the arm and smiled.

"You better take good care of our Nikki, or you will have to answer to Dean and me," Justin said firmly, glancing at Nikki.

"Damn, Justin, Nikki is better off with me anyway. I won't leave her all lonely in a bar like you and Dean do." Chance laughed.

"Nikki knows us. If she were uncomfortable with you, we would stay with her. But Nikki looks rather comfortable with you," Justin winked at Chance, then walked away. Chance shook his head, laughing.

"The two are such male whores." Nikki stated.

"Yes, they are. When I was in the Air Force, I partied a lot with them. Every weekend was always someone new to screw." Chance chuckled.

"There are a lot of military bunnies around to fuck. They are never without a woman, that is for sure." Nikki shook her head in disgust. Chance nodded his head in agreement.

"Yeah, that is true. I am no longer into that scene." Chance remarked.

"Not into military bunnies or fucking?" Nikki glanced over at him smiling.

"Military bunnies. I still like fucking a lot." Chance said seductively.

"Great, because I like fucking too," Nikki replied seductively.

"Well, we have something in common besides being in the Air Force and being airmen." Chance leaned over, whispering in her ear.

"Airwomen." Nikki smiled.

"That you are all women."

"Are you interested, Chance?" Nikki asked softly and hopefully.

"Are you?" Chance replied.

"Oh yes, very interested," Nikki replied.

"It has been a long time since I meet a woman with the same interests as me."

"I understand fully. I haven't been in a relationship or found anybody in a couple of years. The last one was not a good match at all."

"Same here. Being in the Air Force didn't help because I never knew how long I would be stateside. So, I stayed away from any long-term relationships."

"I understand that, plus women want their men to be around all the time."

"You don't want your man around all the time?"

"No, I am not a clingy woman. Being in the Air Force like you, I don't actually make a commitment to anybody except one time I did. We even were engaged. He ended up being married with children."

"Ouch!"

"Yeah, I was not very happy when I found out. I came home because I decided to end my career in the Air Force and didn't tell him. I wanted to surprise him, and did I ever when I showed up at his house."

"Let me guess, the wife answered the door."

"Yes, of course. Then a child showed up tugging her pant leg."

"Ouch, what happened?"

"I just told her I must have had the wrong address because I was looking for my fiancée."

"Did she ask you his name?"

"Yes, she did. I told her, and she called him to the door. Boy, was he shocked seeing me there. He wanted to ask how I found out where he lived."

"Damn!"

"He tried to talk, but I walked away before I said shit in front of his child."

"Great job. I hate guys who cheat. I never cheat. If I am with someone, they are the only one I am with, period."

"I am glad you are honest."

"Don't believe in cheating or lying. Besides, neither will end up in anything good."

"Chance, I think I am liking you more and more."

"I feel the same."

"How about we go back out on the dance floor? The night here is almost coming to an end."

"Sounds great." Chance stood up and held out his hand to Nikki.

Nikki grabbed his hand, standing up. They made their way back to the dance floor. Chance once again pulled her into his arms, bodies swaying together.

Chance felt her body relax into his. Nikki fit against him perfectly. Chance slid his hand down her lower back, pressing her close as he ground his hips against hers. Nikki could feel his hard erection against her pelvis. She was glad he felt as turned on as her. Nikki's whole body seemed alive with desire for this sexy man. She didn't want the night to end.

Nikki finally met a man she could be very interested in, not only sexually but personally. Her mind said to take things slowly, but her body hummed for something more. It had been more than six months since she had been sexually active. Her body was primed and ready for

Chance to take. Their bodies swaying and rubbing against one another wasn't helping the situation either.

Chance bent his head slightly and inhaled her scent of roses and woman. He nuzzled her neck and felt Nikki shiver against him. Chance smiled and lightly slid his tongue up the side of her neck. Nikki's skin broke out in goosebumps as he heard her quick gasp.

"Nikki, you smell delicious." Chance whispered.

"Um...it's....wild roses," Nikki said breathlessly.

"Are you a wild rose, Nikki?"

"When I want to be."

"I like wild sometimes."

The song ended. Nikki felt a wave of disappointment run through her. Then she remembered Chase was supposed to drive her home. They were still on the dance floor with their arms wrapped around each other. Chance looked down at her with a smile.

"The song ended. I guess we need to move off the dance floor." Chance whispered.

"That is a shame because I like it right where I am."

"So do I." Chance's eyes were glued to her lips. He started to bend his head down. Nikki tightened her arms around his neck, tilting her head up. Chance's eyes locked on hers. Nikki moistened her lips. Chance growled in his throat and captured her mouth with his.

Chance couldn't stop after seeing her pink tongue come out and run over her lip, making them wet. Chance ran his tongue over her bottom lip, and she opened her lips for him to swipe his tongue inside. Their tongues gently met, then tangled together in a heated kiss. Chance devoured her mouth until Nikki was breathless. They stood on the dance floor making out, not caring who was watching. Someone hit Chance on the arm.

"Hey, go get a room." The male voice stated.

Chance pulled his mouth from Nikki's, realizing they were still in the middle of the dance floor. Nikki's eyes were filled with desire looking up at him with wet swollen lips. Nikki signed in contentment. Chance looked over his shoulder at the person who had hit his arm.

"Excuse me?" Chance said.

"I said, go get a room. You two are out in the middle of the dance floor, making out like teenagers." The man said, annoyed.

Chance looked down at Nikki's satisfied face and started laughing. They both looked over at the annoyed man.

"Sounds like a plan," They both replied, then busted out laughing. The man shook his head in disgust.

"You two are old enough to act better than teenagers in a public place," The man stated, walking away.

"Sorry man, we don't get out much," Chance yelled at the man. The man stopped and turned around.

"Maybe you better learn then instead of making a scene." The man said.

"Sorry, the wife here doesn't like to leave the babies at home?" Chance replied, smiling.

"Whatever," The main said, waving his hand and dismissing them.

Nikki laughed harder and poked Chance in the ribs. Chance laughed, grabbing her hand and pulling her off the dance floor.

"We should probably go," Chance said, smiling.

"Yes, I am more than ready," Nikki replied, smiling.

"After you, sexy lady."

Nikki smiled and then started walking to the entrance. Chance checked out her sweet ass as she walked in front of him. Nikki's skirt showcased her lovely round ass. She looked over her shoulder at him.

"Chance, are you checking out my ass?" Nikki asked, smiling.

"Yes, I am. You have a sweet round ass," Chance chuckled.

"So do you, by the way, have a nice firm ass," Nikki stated. Chance laughed as they walked outside.

Chapter 4

Chance grabbed her hand as they walked towards the parking lot from the bar. Chance walked to his red Camaro, pushing the key fob to unlock the doors. Chance opened the door for her. Nikki slid inside the car. Chance closed the door, walked around to the driver's side, opened the door, then slid inside.

"Nice car, Chance," Nikki said, smiling.

"Thank you. Where are we going, sexy woman?" Chance asked. Nikki tapped her finger on her lips, thinking. She turned towards him, smiling.

"My place is twenty minutes from here. Are you closer?" Nikki asked.

"I live about ten minutes from here," Chance replied.

"Your place then, or am I being too forward?" Nikki asked hesitantly.

"My place it is," Chance replied, reaching over and squeezing her hand. He put the car into gear and pulled out of the parking lot.

"You are not some serial killer, are you?" Nikki asked, giggling.

"No, I am a lover, not a killer." Chance chuckled, looking over at her grinning and wiggling his eyebrows.

"That is good to know. I wouldn't want to have to mess you up." Nikki gave Chance a serious look. Chance laughed.

"I will let you mess with me, but not mess me up." Chance replied, smiling. Nikki laughed at his comment.

"Chance, did you mention you were in business with your brothers, and are they ex-military also?"

"Yes, I am part owner with them. My brother Carter was in Black Ops. Chase was a Navy SEAL, and Colin was a Marine."

"Holy shit, your brothers were in elite groups in the military."

"Yes, but it was secretive. My brothers don't tell people what they did or the group they belonged to."

"I am sure it was a need-to-know basis."

"Carter was in Black Ops for eight years and still would be. He had to retire from injuries he received from a mission. He was the one to open up Black Security."

"That is great he did something with his training."

"With Black Security, we all use a lot of military training. We install top of line security systems in homes and businesses. We also are being hired for protection."

"That is so cool."

Chance pulled into his driveway. He opened the garage door and drove the car inside, closing the door behind him. Chance climbed out of the car and walked around the passenger side. He opened the door for Nikki and held his hand out. He helped her out of the car. Nikki stepped out of the car.

Nikki followed Chance into the house. She was surprised at how clean and uncluttered the inside of the house was. The kitchen was spotless, and the countertops sparkled. Nikki slid her high heel shoes off, setting them by the door. Chance had taken his boots off already.

"Nikki, would you like some wine or beer?"

"Beer is fine, thank you."

"You can make yourself comfortable in the living room while I get us a beer." Chance said, walking into the kitchen. Nikki nodded her head. She walked through the entryway that led to the living room. Again, she was surprised by his cleanness.

The living room had white walls and white carpet. The furniture was all black leather. There was an 80-inch TV on the wall and a stereo in the corner. The end tables and coffee table had a glass top, spot-free of smudges.

There was nothing in the living room out of place. Nikki sat down on the sofa. She heard Chance moving around in the kitchen. Nikki smiled when the soft music began playing on the TV screen. Chance showed up with the bottles of beer in his hand.

"Here you go." Chance handed her the bottle of beer.

"Thank you," Nikki replied, taking a quick sip. Chance sat down next to her. She glanced over at him smiling.

"Do you have a cleaning lady?" Nikki asked curiously.

"No, I don't. I don't like messiness."

"You are definitely a clean man. Your house is clean and beautiful, nicely decorated."

"Thank you, I think." Chance smiled uncertainly. Nikki laughed at his look of uncertainness.

"I am serious." Nikki smiled. Chance nodded his head.

They were quiet for several minutes listening to the music and sipping their beer. Nikki couldn't stand the silence.

"Chance, what did you do in the Air Force?"

"I flew the rescue helicopter in Afghanistan to pick up injured military men."

"You flew right into the war zones, then?" Nikki asked with curiosity, turning to her side to face him.'

"Yes, I did. I have a bullet hole in my shoulder and arm from the returned fire to remind me."

"Were you over there the whole time of enlistment?"

"Pretty much. I went over after I passed the training."

"You were one of the lucky ones to come back whole."

"Came back complete but not without scars."

"Do you have dreams of being over there?"

"Yeah, sometimes I still do. Not as much now as when I first came back."

"Was your helicopter ever shot down?"

"Yes, it was a few times, but of course, not fatally."

"I never got a chance to go over there, thank god."

"I am glad. It was a hell hole. You need another beer?"

"Sure."

Chance stood up and walked to the kitchen. He was glad to have something to do. He preferred to avoid talking about Afghanistan. Chance couldn't believe he had answered Nikki's questions. He usually tried to change the subject to something else. Chance grabbed a couple more beers from the fridge. He walked back to the sofa and handed Nikki another beer. Nikki took the beer from him and smiled.

"Thank you, I am sorry if I made you uncomfortable with my questions."

"You are fine. It just is hard to talk about sometimes." Chance sat down beside her again on the sofa. They quiet for a few more minutes.

"Chance, I want to see your battle wounds," Nikki asked softly.

Chance glanced over at her, then pulled his short-sleeved shirt up to his shoulder. Nikki noticed the Air Force tattoo on his bicep. The bullet scar was just above it on his upper arm.

Nikki reached over, tracing it with her fingertip. She then bent her head down, kissing the scar. Chance shivered at her warm, light touch of her lips on his arm. He had never had a woman kiss his scar before. Chance felt the soft touch of her tongue swirl around the scar.

Chance glanced down at her. Nikki was looking up at him. Their eyes locked, and their mouths came together quickly in a fever of hunger. Chance ran his tongue over her bottom lip. She opened it and let him inside. Their tongues tangle and twist together, tasting.

Chance turned his body towards her and deepened the kiss. Her hand fisted the front of his t-shirt while her other hand pressed against the back of his neck, holding him to her mouth. Their tongues tasted and mated with passion.

Nikki moaned in his mouth. Chance reached over and pulled Nikki onto his lap. She pressed her body close to his, feeling his heat.

Her breasts were crushed against his chest. Nikki licked and sucked his tongue.

Nikki let loose of his neck, tangling her fingers in his hair. Chance slid his hand up her leg from knee to upper thigh, caressing her bare leg. His other hand held her head, fingers tangling in her hair firmly as his mouth ravished hers.

His tongue tasted hers thoroughly until they both were breathless. Nikki could feel his hard erection pressed against her thigh and knew he was as turned on as her. Nikki wiggled on his lap, trying to get closer. She heard Chance moan as she rubbed against his hard bulge.

Chance pulled his mouth from hers and looked into her with desire-filled eyes. Nikki's eyes were half-mass as she stared back at him. Her tongue came out, and she licked her bottom lip.

"More Chance, I want more of you," Nikki whispered. Chance grinned at her and gently pushed her onto her back. Nikki wrapped her arms around his neck, pulling him down to her.

Chance's back was against the back of the sofa. Nikki rested her legs on his hip. He turned his body sideways and captured her mouth once again. His left hand began a heated trail from her thigh to her rib cage. Chance stopped his hand just underneath her breast.

Nikki moaned in his mouth for his hand to continue its journey upwards. Chance smiled against her lips. He slowly moved his hand up, cupping and molding her large breasts. Chance's fingers felt her nipples grow hard under his touch. His fingertips caressed circles around the hard nubs.

Nikki arched her back, giving him better access. His fingers left and started to unbutton her blouse. One by one, the buttons came undone under his fingers. Nikki felt the cool air on her skin as Chance moved her blouse to the side.

His firm, hot hands left a heated trail wherever he caressed her bare skin, the tops of her breasts and stomach. His mouth left hers. His hot tongue blazed a wet path up the side of her neck around the shell of her ear. Nikki shivered, skin breaking out in goosebumps.

Chance's fingers worked the clasp of her bra, freeing her breasts from their confines. He moved the bra cups out of the way. Chance's large hand lifted and caressed her large breasts, touching every inch of them. Her breasts felt hot from his hands. His fingers pinched and touched her nipples into stiff peaks.

Chance loved the feel of her heavy breasts under his palms. Her breasts overfilled his hands. Nikki's breasts had to be double D or E cups. Her nipples were large and pink. Chance couldn't wait any longer to taste the large globes.

Chance gently lifted the heavy globes, bent his head, and buried his face in the softness. His mouth and tongue tasted every inch of her luscious breasts, leaving a wet hot trail behind. Her breasts tasted fruity from her lotion. Chance smiled, thinking of watermelons because of the size and heaviness of her breasts.

Chance really didn't care for watermelon, but he loved hers. He could spend all day on her breast and be content. Nikki was wiggling and moaning underneath him. Chance pulled his mouth from her breasts, glancing up at her with a grin.

"God, Nikki, I love your beautiful tits. They taste fruity and are delicious."

"You don't think they are too big?"

"Hell no. They are beautiful with large pink, rosy nipples to fill a man's mouth."

"I have always been self-conscious of my boobs."

"Why?" Chance asked, sucking her nipple into his mouth and staring at her. Nikki moaned, watching him feast on her nipple.

"I...used to get....oh god...teased from being so big."

Nikki's breath came out in pants as his mouth sucked harder on her nipple. His other hand pinched her other nipple. Nikki's body jerked from having her nipples pinched and sucked simultaneously. A light pulsing ache began inside pussy, making her arousal grow stronger.

Chance gently bit down on her nipple and pinched the other one harder. Her tongue moistened her dry lips and then caught her bottom lip between her teeth. Chance's cock pushed hard against his zipper, watching her pink tongue slide over her bottom lip. His mouth let go of her nipple with a pop sound. Chance watched her eyes widen and darken in response.

"Nikki, don't ever feel self-conscious of having beautiful tits. Men love having more than a mouth full to play with."

"Mine are definitely more than a mouthful. My boobs definitely get looked at more than my face since they enter the room first."

"Not true. I noticed your beautiful face first."

"Really?"

"Yes, I didn't notice your beautiful tits until you stood up to dance with me."

"Honestly?"

"Honest to God." Chance grinned, making a cross over his heart. Nikki laughed at the jester.

" Now I want to see yours."

Chance grinned and sat up. He reached down, grabbed the hem of his t-shirt, and pulled it over his head, tossing it on the floor. Nikki's eyes widened, looking at his broad, muscular smooth chest. His flat stomach was ribbed with muscle showing off a perfect six-pack of abs.

Nikki reached out, running her hand over the warm, smooth muscle. She was fascinated with how his muscles rippled and moved under her fingertips. His chest muscles twitched as her fingers circled his flat dark nipples.

"God, you are hard and soft at the same time."

"I try to keep in shape since I am no longer in the Air Force."

"I do, too. I love yoga."

"See another thing we have in common, keeping in shape."

"I am glad. This night just keeps getting better and better."

"How much better do you what it to be, Nikki?"

Nikki smiled at him, then raised her head, taking his lips in a heated kiss and answering his question. Their tongues tangled in desire while their hands caressed each other. Chance moved his hand down her legs, brushing from knee to upper thigh.

Nikki felt Chance's hand slide underneath the hem of her skirt. Chance slowly slid his hand up, taking her skirt with him. His hand slid over her silky skin, leaving a hot trail behind. Nikki trembled as his hand inched higher and higher toward her burning desire.

Chance's fingers followed the leg seam of her panties. Nikki knew he would feel the dampness on her panties from her arousal. Her core throbbed with anticipation of his fingers so close to her need. His finger slid underneath the seam of her panties traveling around to the front. Nikki moved her legs apart a little more to give him better access.

Chance's finger moved down between her legs, following the seam of her panties. His finger slid down between her inner thigh and pussy. Chance could feel the dampness of her arousal on her panties. He didn't touch her pussy yet, just wanting to tease her more.

Chance felt her legs tremble and her hips raise up. He knew Nikki was trying to get his finger to her pussy. He could feel her heat and smell her arousal. Chance slid his finger along the crease of her inner thigh and pussy, feeling her bare soft silky skin. Nikki moaned in his mouth. His hand slipped further underneath her panties, caressing and squeezing her ass cheeks.

Chance moved his hand out from underneath her panties and skirt. Nikki groaned at the loss of his hand. Chance moved his hand to the zipper on the side of her skirt, pulling the zipper down. His hand moved to the waistband of her skirt, pushing it down. Nikki let go of his neck, reaching down, pushing, and wiggling out of her skirt.

Nikki dropped the skirt on the floor next to the sofa. Chance slid his hand under the waistband of her panties, moving straight down to her pussy. Nikki shivered in delight. Her core throbbed more intensely for his attention. His hand cupped her bare pussy.

Nikki's hips jerked forward. His finger slid between her wet folds, getting a gasp from her mouth. Chance sucked her tongue as his finger pressed inside her wet opening. His tongue and finger moved in rhythm together, moving in and out.

Chance's finger became slick from her arousal, moving in and out of her. He pulled his mouth from hers, and looking into her desire-filled eyes, he whispered against her mouth.

"I want to taste your cream." Chance pumped his finger inside her, thumb rubbing against her swollen clit. She groaned against her lips.

"Yes."

Chance's lips and tongue traveled down her neck to her breast, leaving a wet, tingling trail on her heated skin. Nikki's body wiggled underneath him. He stopped at her breasts, playing and sucking her nipples. Chance bit her nipple and pinched her clit, simultaneously sliding his finger into her slick opening.

"Jeezus, Chance!" Nikki groaned as her hips jerked and her clit throbbed harder with need.

Nikki's walls clenched his finger driving it deeper inside her. Her body trembled with a need for release. Chance let go of her nipple, raising his head and staring at her.

"Don't you dare cum yet. I want your cream on my tongue. I want to taste your honey," Chance demanded. Nikki nodded her head, moaning loudly and biting her bottom lip.

"Hurry, I am on edge, Chance."

Chance pulled his finger out of her and then pulled her panties off her. He dropped them on the floor with the rest of their clothes. Nikki was now naked on the sofa underneath his big body.

Chance raised up, staring at her beautiful naked body with hunger. He grabbed her legs, spreading them and moving between them. He raised her legs to each shoulder, kissing her ankles. Chance bent his head and buried his face like a starved man between her legs.

Chance flattened his tongue, swiping the entire length of her bare pussy a couple of times. He latched onto her clit, licking and sucking it into his mouth until it was swollen and stiff, getting a loud gasp from Nikki. Chance let go of her clit and buried his tongue inside her wet channel. His tongue swirled and twisted inside of her. He moved his tongue in and out of her.

Nikki's body trembled in pleasure. She moaned and started to move her hips with his rhythm. Chance slid his hands under her ass. He pushed her ass up higher as his tongue drove deeper inside her. His tongue fucked her faster as her wall clenched him harder in need. He moved one hand out from beneath her.

Chance brought his hand up and started to pinch and roll her clit between his fingers. Nikki moaned loudly as she began to come. His lips and tongue were slick with her arousal. Chance could taste her sweet cream coating his tongue.

Chance slowed down his tongue as she trembled underneath him. He pulled his tongue out of her. Chance kissed her pussy and then kissed her way up her body. He captured her mouth. She sucked his tongue, tasting herself on his tongue, driving her wild with the need to be filled by him.

Nikki's hands moved down to his jeans. She unbuttoned and unzipped his jeans. Nikki's hand slid inside his jeans. His cock was hard and stiff against her hand. Her hand wrapped firmly around his shaft. Nikki started to firmly stroke his hard cock. He growled in her mouth with pleasure. Nikki removed her hand from his hard cock. Nikki pulled her mouth from his. She smiled at him seductively.

"My turn to drive you crazy with need," Nikki whispered.

Nikki then moved so he was on his back, and she was on top of him. She slid down his body, kissing his chest. Her tongue swirled and sucked on his nipples until they were hard. She kissed and licked her way down to his stomach. His stomach muscles rippled under her tongue and lips. Nikki's hands caressed their way down his body, following her mouth. Nikki dipped her tongue into his belly button. Her hands moved to the waistband of his jeans.

"Your jeans need to come off. I want to see and taste all of you." Nikki smiled.

"Let's take this to my bedroom." Chance whispered. Nikki nodded her head.

Nikki slid off him, standing up next to the sofa. Chance sat up, slipping off the sofa. He stood up, holding his hand out to her. Nikki put her hand in his and followed him down the hallway to his bedroom. Chance opened the door to his bedroom. The light in the bedroom was dim. Nikki glanced around the dim room.

"Nice and clean," Nikki laughed. Chance smiled and then kissed her lips. He stared at her with hunger.

"Damn, you are so fucking beautiful," Chance whispered, cupping her face in his hands.

"So are you. Now take those jeans off so I can see the rest of you naked." Nikki said seductively. Chance laughed.

"You wish is my command," Chance said, sliding his jeans off. He pushed down his boxers. Nikki's eyes widened in hunger, looking at him. Nikki's eyes traveled the entire length of his nice hard, toned muscular body. Chance was a big man in all the right places.

Chance's body was muscular with a perfect V-line. His abs rippled with muscle into a perfect six-pack. His huge cock stood straight up to his navel. He was a magnificent male.

"Do you like what you see, Nikki?"

"Oh yeah, you are one hot beautiful man."

"Well, I don't know about beautiful, but I am glad you approve. The way you are checking me out, I was scared for a minute that I didn't pass." Chance chuckled.

"Oh, I approve, and yes, you pass with flying colors." Nikki slid down to her knees in front of him. She looked up at him, smiling wickedly. "Chance, have you ever fucked a woman's mouth?" Chance chuckled.

"I am a thirty-year-old man. I have had many blowjobs in my time."

"No, not a blowjob. I want you to fuck my mouth like you would my pussy."

"Okay, if that is what you want."

"Oh yes, I want your cock sliding in and out deep inside my mouth." Nikki nodded her head.

She grabbed his cock into her hand, stroking him a few times, then ran her tongue over his shaft. Her tongue swirled over the mushroom head several times.

"Now fuck my mouth, Airman." Nikki opened her mouth wide and cupped his ass cheeks, pulling him closer.

Chance reached out, cupping her jaw with one hand. He grabbed his cock, positioning it at the opening of her mouth. He rubbed the head of his cock over his lips, spreading the pre-cum over them. Chance slowly slipped his cock inside her opened mouth. He groaned at the feel of his cock sliding over her wet hot tongue.

Nikki tightened her mouth to hold his cock firmly inside her mouth. Chance started to pump his hips back and forth. His cock slipped in and out of her wet hot mouth. She moaned around his cock, sending vibrations up his spine.

"God, baby, is this what you want?" Chance growled out, moving back and forth a little faster.

Nikki hummed around his cock. She grabbed his ass, pushing him inside of her mouth deeper. His cock hit the back of her throat then she swallowed him. Chance felt her throat muscles clench his cock tightly.

"Holy shit, Nikki," Chance growled.

His cock swelled inside her mouth. Nikki's tongue rubbed back and forth on the underside of his cock. She kept swallowing, making her throat muscles massage the head of his cock.

"Baby, I will explode in your mouth if you don't let loose." Chance growled.

Chance tried to back out of her mouth a little, but Nikki held his ass firmly in her hands, not letting him move. She swallowed again, then hummed. The vibrations set him on fire. Chance's balls drew close to his body, and his cock jerked inside her mouth. He pumps his hips faster in a short pump, feeling the tingling sensations running down his spine straight to his balls. Nikki worked her throat muscles, squeezing his cock tighter.

"Fuck!" Chance growled as his cum exploded inside her mouth.

Chance's orgasm was so intense his legs almost buckled, and his toes curled from the force. Nikki kept swallowing as he came inside her mouth. She let loose so he could pull out after emptying himself down her throat. Nikki slowly slid her mouth up his cock and licked him clean. She stood up with a wicked grin.

"Damn, woman, that was fucking amazing. But now you are going to have to wait for me to recover. I came hard in your mouth. I thought my cock would split in two," Chance said breathlessly.

"I promise to make you come hard again," Nikki said seductively, then pushed him back so he landed on the bed. Chance laughed. Nikki was a wild one.

"This will not take long before you are hard and ready to go again."

"Oh yeah, now what are you going to do to me?" Chance asked, smiling.

"I am going to get you hard and make you come hard again."

"Is that so," Chance chuckled.

"Promise." Nikki climbed up on the bed between his legs on her knees.

She bent her head down and buried her face in his balls. She was glad to see Chance man-scaped. Her hot wet tongue slid over his bare balls, leaving a wet path. She gently fondled them with her hand as her tongue massaged and sucked. Nikki sucked his smooth balls hard to almost painful. Chance watched her with hunger as his balls moved in and out of her mouth.

Chance felt her wet finger slide up the crack of his ass and probe his hole. As she sucked his balls, her finger began to push inside his hole. Chance tensed a bit, never having someone play with his asshole before. It was sort of uncomfortable but yet arousing. Nikki continued to lick and suck his balls as her finger slipped inside his virgin hole.

Chance growled as her finger began to move in and out. The pleasure /pain aroused him further. His cock stiffen to full mass. Nikki hooked her finger and stroked his prostate, sending white-hot tingles to his balls.

"Fuck, Nikki!" Chance growled in pleasure. Nikki let loose his balls and gently pulled her finger out of his ass. She crawled and straddled his hips, rubbing her wet sex against his hard cock.

"Did you like that?" Nikki smiled.

"You are the first that has ever tried that."

"I told you I could get you hard quickly."

"Yes, you did."

"Where do you hide your condoms?"

Chance reached over to the drawer beside the bed and opened it. He grabbed out a packet. Nikki took the condom from his hand. She smiled at him, opening the condom and putting it into her mouth. Nikki rolled the condom on his cock with her mouth. Chance laughed.

"You, baby, are full of surprises."

"You ready to be rode, cowboy?"

"Bring it on, cowgirl."

Nikki rose on her knees, grabbed his stiff cock, and positioned it at her entrance. Nikki slowly slid down on his stiff cock as he raised his hips, pushing inside her. His huge cock slowly stretched her out as he entered her slick wet channel. Nikki wiggled on him as his cock stretched her to fit his size. Chance stayed still when he was entirely inside her so she could adjust to him. They both moaned at being joined.

"Damn, baby, you feel amazing," Chance groaned.

"So do you," Nikki moaned out as she began to move up and down on his stiff cock.

Nikki braced her hands on his chest to balance herself as she rode his cock up and down. Chance reached down, gripping her ass cheeks as she rode him faster. Her body slammed down as he pushed up hard with his hips. They both were breathless. Chance sat up, wrapping his arms around her waist. Nikki wiggled and ground on his cock. Chance felt her wall clenching his cock in need.

Chance quickly rolled them over. He pulled out of her and then flipped Nikki onto her stomach. Nikki got up on her hands and knees. Chance moved behind her spread legs and quickly entered her wet channel in one thrust. Nikki gasped out in pleasure. Chance put his hands on her hips and started to pound fast in and out of her.

"Fuck, yeah, Chance. Oh yes!" Nikki moaned.

"Damn, you are tight," Chance panted, quickly moving in and out of her.

Chance pulled his cock almost out and then quickly slammed back inside her hard and fast. His thumb circled her asshole. Nikki pushed back against his thumb and moaned yes. Chance knew then she wanted his thumb inside her ass. He slowly pushed inside her ass with his thumb as he buried his cock deep inside her.

"Fuck, yes, right there," Nikki growled loudly.

Chance felt her walls clench hard as she started to cum. He moved his thumb in and out of her ass like his cock did inside her pussy. She was so slick. He slipped in and out of her with ease. Chance shorted his strokes, feeling her cum all over his cock. Chance growled as he started to cum inside her, pulling his thumb out.

Chance pumped in and out of her until he was empty. Chance slapped her ass hard a few times before he pulled out of her. Nikki moaned and collapsed down on the bed breathing heavily. Chance pulled out of her and laid on his back next to her. He was breathing hard. His hand came up and rubbed his chest over his fast-beating heart.

"Damn, Nikki, I think I am spent." Chance chuckled, looking over at her grinning.

"I am, too, for a few hours," Nikki said, giggling. Chance glanced over at the clock. It was 2:00am. He didn't feel like moving to take her home.

"Nikki, do you want to stay, or am I taking you home?"

"What time is it?" Nikki asked, yawning.

"It is 2:00am."

"I'll stay if that is all right with you? I am quite comfortable right now and don't want to move."

"Great, because I don't want to move yet either." Chance pulled the used condom off and tossed it into the trash can beside the bed. They moved and climbed under the covers. Nikki snuggled up to Chance's side.

"Chance, I don't usually make a habit of sleeping with men I just met," Nikki said sincerely.

"I am glad. I don't make a habit of sleeping with men either," Chance replied, snickering. Nikki pinched his nipple.

"Ouch!" Chance yelped and rubbed his nipple.

"There is something about you that gets me all riled up," Nikki said, smiling.

"The same with me. I usually don't bring women home."

"Good to know."

Chance bent his head and captured her lips in a passionate kiss. Their tongues slid against each other, tangled and twisted in desire for a few minutes before parting. Nikki rolled over on her side. Chance snuggled up to her back. They soon fell fast asleep.

Chapter 5

When Nikki woke up the following morning, Chance was gone from the bed. Nikki heard the shower going. She stretched and sat up in the bed. Nikki knew her clothes were on the living room floor where their little party had started. She smiled, feeling the little bit of soreness between her legs. God, Chance had been a remarkable lover last night.

Chance came walking into the bedroom with a towel wrapped around his hips and a grin. He saw her sitting up in his bed. Chance grinned and winked at her.

"Damn, you look good in my bed with your tousled hair and bright eyes," Chance smiled, wiggling his eyebrows seductively.

"You look sexy as hell wearing just a towel." Nikki licked her lips, letting the bed sheet fall from her covered breasts. Chance's eyes darkened, staring at her large bare breasts.

"Don't look at me like that, or you will never get out of my bed today," Chance started walking towards her with a huge grin.

"I cannot leave your bed. I don't have any clothes. I think they are still in the living room," Nikki giggled.

"I will go get them. You can take a shower if you want or wait in the bed for me." Chance said subjectively and grinned. Nikki laughed.

"Thanks, I think I will." Nikki grinned.

"Which one, take a shower or wait for me in the bed naked?" Chance asked seductively.

"I guess you have to wait and see when you get back," Nikki giggled.

Chance walked out to the living room. Nikki's clothes were on the floor where they had left them last night. Chance bent down to pick up Nikki's clothes when someone knocked on the door. Chance walked to the door holding Nikki's panties in his hand, opening the door. Chase was standing on the porch.

"Hey, Chance, did I catch you at a bad time?" Chase asked, looking at a pair of woman's panties dangling from Chance's finger and wearing a towel around his hips.

"No, why?" Chance asked, puzzled.

"You have a pair of woman's panties dangling from your hand and wearing a bath towel." Chase laughed. Chance glanced down, forgetting he was getting Nikki's clothes for her and had a towel around his hips.

"Shit, Nikki is in the bedroom or shower. Come on in, Chase."

"Who is Nikki?" Chase asked, walking into the house.

"Nikki is a friend of Justin and Dean's and is also an ex-Air Force I met last night." Chance laughed, picking up the rest of Nikki's clothes from the floor.

"Looks like you had quite a fun party last night. This Nikki must be special because you never have women here," Chase smiled, and Chance laughed.

"I know what you are saying. It was an instant attraction. I just met her, but I already like Nikki a lot. We have a lot in common, and she is also a pilot. I'll be right back," Chance said, holding Nikki's clothes. Chase nodded his head.

Chance walked towards the bedroom with the rest of Nikki's clothes. He opened the door, stepping inside. Nikki was still sitting in his bed with a huge grin and bare breasts showing. Chance groaned in disappointment. Nikki gave him the come-to hinder finger, tossing the rest of the blankets off her luscious naked body.

"Damn, you look sexy as fucking hell, babe."

"Come here and give me some more of your hot body." Nikki licked her lip, then caught her bottom between her teeth. Chance moved closer to the bed and shook his head with regret.

"Fuck Nik, I wish I could, but my brother Chase is here."

"Shit, did he see my clothes all over your living room." Nikki grabbed the blankets covering herself back up. Chance climbed on the bed, pulling the blankets down under his breasts. He reached out, cupping her heavy breasts.

"Yes, Chase did, plus I am wearing a towel." Chance pointed to the towel that was tented with his erection. Nikki snickered.

"You didn't answer the door with a huge hard-on, did you?"

"No, you just gave me one showing me these magnificent tits of yours." Chance bent his head down, sucking her nipple into his mouth. Her nipple instantly hardened in his mouth.

"Chance, stop. Your brother is waiting for you." Nikki said, grabbing his short hair and pulling.

Chance sucked harder on her nipple. His other hand cupped and molded the other breasts. Nikki moaned, feeling the wetness between her legs.

"Chance!" Nikki moaned, pulling his hair harder. Chance growled, letting loose her nipple.

"Damn, Nik, I can smell your arousal. You are wet for me, aren't you?" Chance reached underneath the covers burying his hand between her legs, finding her wetness. He slipped his finger between her wet folds. Nikki moaned, grabbed his hand, and pulled it away from her aching pussy.

"Yes, but your brother is here. You need to get dressed."

"Fuck, babe," Chance brought his finger to his mouth, then sucked her essence off. Nikki licked her lip and moaned, watching him lick his finger.

"Get dressed, and I am going to shower," Nikki stated. Chance lowered his head, kissing her breasts. Her nipples were dark pink and poking out from his mouth.

"Damn, I hate to see you cover up my twins." Chance said with a pouty lip. Nikki laughed and swatted him on the shoulder.

"They happen to be my twins. Now leave them alone and get dressed before your brother comes in here to see what's taking you so long."

"Chase better not because I will not share these beauties." Chance smiled, cupping and squeezing her breasts again. Nikki swatted his hand.

"Hands off the twins, mister."

"Damn it." Chance let loose her breasts and moved off the bed. Chance stood up, then dropped the towel from his hips, baring his naked body to her. He heard Nikki gasp behind him and smiled.

"Nik, you better not be staring at my ass."

"You have a great firm ass."

"I'll give you something to stare at that is more impressive." Chance turned around. Nikki's mouth dropped open with an O forming on her lips. Chance's cock stood straight up to his navel.

"That looks a little painful." Nikki giggled, seeing the sad look on his face.

"It really hurts, babe," Chance said, reaching down and stroking his cock a few times, grimacing.

Nikki licked her suddenly dry lips. Her eyes locked on his hand, stroking his stiff cock. Chance snickered. Nikki looked up at his smiling face and pointed her finger at him.

"Stop teasing me and get dressed," Nikki said. Chance and Nikki busted up laughing, hearing Chase holler out to Chance.

"Chance, get your ass out here." Chase hollered. Chance let loose of his cock and pulled on a pair of boxers, groaning in frustration.

"Damn brothers, they always show up at the wrong time." Chance pulled on a pair of jeans, tucking his hard-on inside and zipping up his pants with a grimace. Nikki giggled, watching Chance pout and tuck his huge hard-on into his jeans. Chance looked over at her and shook his head.

"Damn, brother." Chance muttered, walking towards the bedroom door. He looked over his shoulder at her again, regretfully shaking his head. Nikki laughed even harder at his expression.

"Poor baby," Nikki said, laughing louder as he walked out of the bedroom, closing the door. Chance walked back out to the kitchen. Chase was sitting in the kitchen corner.

Chase gave Chance a huge smile, shaking his head in disbelief. This was Chase's first time seeing his brother with a woman in a while.

"Need some coffee?" Chance asked.

"Sure; what does Nikki do now since she is out of the Air Force?"

"She has a cargo business. Nikki flies all over delivering supplies for her clients." Chance grabbed a couple of coffee cups and poured them both a cup of coffee. He slid a cup to Chase.

"That is great; she has her own business," Chase said, sipping the coffee.

"Nikki owns her own plane."

"Does she have a lot of clients?"

"I am not sure. We only got into a few details.

"Too busy twisting up the sheets." Chase laughed. Chance laughed, punching Chase in the arm.

"I am sure you and Jaci do a lot of twisting the sheets between concerts."

"Hell, yes. Especially since we only see each other once a month. Would your friend be interested in flying me out every other weekend?

"Nikki might. I don't know her schedule."

Nikki got dressed and walked out to the kitchen. Nikki heard another male voice in the kitchen. Chance and Chase turned, looking at Nikki as she walked towards them. Nikki couldn't believe how gorgeous the man was sitting at the counter.

Chase had blonde curly hair and bright blue eyes. He had Chance's dimples while smiling at her. For some reason, he looked familiar to her. Then the closer she got, Chase reminded her of the actor Paul

Walker from the "Fast and Furious" movies. He was hot, but she thought Chance was more seductive.

"Nikki, this is my brother, Chase," Chance said, waving his hand at Chase.

"Hello, Chase," Nikki smiled.

"Would you like some coffee?" Chance asked. Nikki nodded her head to him. She kept looking at Chase, smiling.

"You have probably seen Chase in the tabloids. He is dating Jaci Hurst, the rock singer," Chance chuckled.

"No shit. I like Jaci's music. Jaci has a raspy, sultry voice. I thought you were Paul Walker at first glance," Nikki said, smiling. Chase groaned, and Chance laughed at her comment.

"No, not Paul Walker. When I first met Jaci, she always called me Paul Walker's twin. Now she does it just to irritate me. Jaci has a sultry voice. I am not into much rock, but her singing is a turn-on for me."

"You were the one that helped catch her stalker."

"Yes, I was. I was hired to be Jaci's bodyguard. Her stalker ended up being her manager. The sick son of a bitch," Chase stated firmly in disgust.

"I heard they want to do a movie about Jaci's ordeal."

"Yes, there has been talk about it. I don't know if Jaci is up to it or not. She has been really busy with touring."

"So, you two have a long-distance relationship going on?"

"Yes, sometimes it gets a little frustrating, but we are working it out. Which reminds me, Chance was saying you have your own plane?"

"Yes, I do." Nikki sat down at the counter next to Chance. Chase noticed Chance grabbed Nikki's hand and twined their fingers together. Chase smiled at his brother.

"Would you be interested in another side job?"

"Doing what?" Nikki asked curiously.

"Flying me to wherever Jaci is every other week."

"I could as long as it doesn't interfere with my deliveries. I have some clients who pay very well to do their deliveries."

"What do you deliver?" Chase asked with curiosity.

"Just about everything, as long is not too heavy or too large for my plane."

"Where do you fly to most of the time?" Chase asked.

"I travel a lot to Mexico, Costa Rica, and Guatemala, depending on who the client is."

Chance and Chase looked at each other with concern. There have been a lot of drugs being flown into those countries lately.

"Nikki, do you inspect your cargo?" Chance asked curiously, looking at her intently.

"Sure, most of it is material, art, electronics, dry goods, and medical supplies," Nikki replied casually, waving her hand.

"I just hope you are very careful." Chance stated. Nikki gave him a puzzled look sipping her coffee. She was slightly uncomfortable with all the questions like they knew something she didn't.

"I don't want to be rude, but this is my business, and I take pride in what I do," Nikki stated firmly.

"I am sorry. I didn't mean to imply anything," Chance replied. Nikki nodded her head.

"Chase, when are you thinking of flying out?" Nikki asked, changing the subject.

"This Thursday, Jaci is in Utah," Chase replied.

"I'll check my schedule when I get home. I believe I might be able to fly you there."

"Great, just call our office. I am there all week," Chase replied, standing up. He looked over at Chance.

"See you tomorrow at work," Chase said.

"Yes, you will." Chance replied, walking with Chase to the front door.

"Nikki is definitely a looker and feisty at that." Chase smiled.

"Yeah, I think so, too," Chance smiled.

"See you later," Chase said, walking out the door. Chance closed the door, walking back into the kitchen. Nikki was still sitting at the counter sipping her coffee.

"I am going to finish getting dressed," Chance said, smiling.

"You don't have to. I like you with no shirt on." Nikki said, reaching out, grabbing the belt loops on his jeans, and pulling Chance to her. Chance stood in front of her with a huge grin.

"I like you with no shirt also." Chance said seductively.

He reached out, cupped, and molded her breasts. Nikki laughed. Chance bent this head down, capturing her mouth in a passionate kiss. Their tongues tangled and twisted together. After thoroughly tasting each other, they pulled apart. Nikki smiled and slapped Chance on the ass.

"Go get a shirt on before I take your pants off," Nikki said, squeezing his ass. Chance laughed, stepping back. He turned and then walked to his bedroom.

Chance grabbed a black t-shirt pulling it on over his head. He sat on the bed, drawing on a pair of socks and his tennis shoes. Once done, he walked back out to the kitchen.

"So, Nikki, what do we do now?"

"Well, I need a ride home to change my clothes. Then I have to check my schedule. I believe I am free the rest of the day."

"So, does that mean you would like to spend the day with me?"

" I would like that very much." Nikki raised her toes, planting a kiss on his lips.

"Well, let's go and see if you are free for Thursday," Chance said, slapping her on the ass.

Chance grabbed his wallet, put it in his back pocket, then grabbed his car keys off the ring. They headed out the side door to the garage. Chance opened the car door for Nikki. Nikki slipped down inside the car, closing the passenger door. Chance walked around the car, opened the driver's side, slipped inside, and closed the door.

"Where to, beautiful?" Chance asked, pulling out onto the road.

"West Chester Village Apartments," Nikki responded.

"Are those the apartment buildings on Sugnet Drive?"

"Yes, they are."

"Those are nice apartments. I looked at them before I bought my house."

" I really enjoy living there. I don't have to worry about taking care of anything."

"That is true. I have to hire a neighbor kid to mow my lawn when I am out of town. That is also why I don't have any pets; otherwise, I would have a dog."

"I have never had a pet. My mother has terrible allergies to any kind of animal hair. So, I was not allowed to have any."

"Do you like animals?" Chance asked. Nikki shrugged her shoulders.

"I guess I do, but I never really thought about it. I never had the urge to go get a pet. I graduated from high school, went to college for four years, and joined the Air Force, so I really didn't have time to take care of a pet."

"So, how old are you?"

"I just turned 30 last month. Why are you going to tell me you are 40 or something?" Nikki laughed. Chance snorted.

"Really, do I look 40?" Chance arched his eyebrow at her. Nikki laughed harder.

"Of course not, but if you were, you would be a very hot, sexy, handsome 40 -year-old."

"I forgive you."

"How old did you think I was?"

"I was hoping you were over 25, or I would feel like I robbed the cradle."

"You didn't rob the cradle. I am of legal age to have sex with a thirty-year-old."

"Thank god, I am thirty-three," Chance laughed, reaching up and rubbing his forehead with his hand. Nikki laughed louder. Chance pulled into the apartment complex parking lot.

"I live at the far end building," Nikki said, pointing towards the end of the building. Chance nodded his head and then pulled into a parking spot. They climbed out of his car, walking towards the building. Chance followed Nikki to her apartment. She unlocked the door, stepping inside with Chance right behind her.

"Make yourself comfortable while go change my clothes," Nikki said, pointing to the sofa. Chance nodded his head and then sat down on the sofa. "Do you want anything to drink while you wait here for me?"

"No, I'm fine, thank you." Chance smiled.

Nikki nodded and then walked to her bedroom to change her clothes. She had been in the middle of sliding her skirt off when she heard Chance's voice.

"Nik, do you need any help getting dressed?" Chance yelled. Nikki laughed, hearing his comment.

"No, I want to change my clothes, not have them taken off."

"Are you sure, babe? I am magnificent at helping."

Nikki came out of the bedroom wearing snug-fitting blue jeans and a white t-shirt that stretched over her lovely large tits. Chance stared at her with a grin.

"Damn, you look fucking hot in jeans."

"Well, thank you. Are you ready to go? I am starving since you didn't feed me breakfast."

"I could feast on you and be happy," Chance said suggestively, wiggling his eyebrows.

"I could feast on you too, but I need food."

"Damn!"

Nikki busted up laughing, walking towards the door. Chance followed her, staring at her sweet round ass. He couldn't resist reaching out, caressing and squeezing her ass.

"Damn, woman, you have a sweet, firm ass."

"So do you, hotness."

"Oh, I like the sound of that." Chance slapped her on the ass as they walked out the door.

They decided to go to lunch at a small deli. They ordered the subs to go and took them to the park to eat. Chance and Nikki sat down on the ground to eat their sandwiches. Chance really felt comfortable with Nikki.

"So, Nikki, tell me about yourself. Who is Nikki Curtis?" Chance asked, smiling.

"Um...let's see. I graduated from high school at the age of 18. My parents died in a car accident shortly after I graduated from high school. They had a lot of debts, so everything they had was sold. I had to learn to grow up fast. I am an only child, and my grandparents were also gone. I had nowhere to go after the state sold my parent's house. So went to live with my mother's sister. She encouraged me to go to college. I got into college on a Pell Grant while working full-time at the local grocery store. I went for four years when I decided that was enough and wanted to join the Air Force program. So I joined the Air Force at the age of 22. I served six years in the Air Force, and now I own my own business here."

"So, you basically have been on your own since you were 18 without much help?"

"Yep, my aunt helped as much as she could, but she was a single woman barely making it by herself. I decided I couldn't continue to burn myself out, going to college full time and working full time. I enlisted in the Air Force for six years. I served six years and decided I could make a lot more money flying independently. I work really hard to get my business up and running smoothly. I learned to depend on no one except myself. If I want to be successful, I have to do it myself.

"How on did you get a cargo plane for your deliveries,"

"I lease the plane with the option to buy."

"Shit, that has to be expensive."

"Um... very, but the deliveries I make for my clients pay the lease payment."

"That is great, but do you have extra left to live on?"

"Yes, Chance, I do very well."

"I am sorry; I know it is not any of my business since we just met."

"You are fine.

"Just tell me to mine my own business."

"Chance, mind your own business," Nikki said, laughing. Chance gave her a huge smile.

"So, it is your turn. Who is Chance Black?"

"Chance Black graduated from high school at 18 and joined the Air Force immediately. I served six years, then signed up for another six years, thinking that going to Afghanistan would be great to fight and kill some terrorists. A war where there are no winners. I have and wear battle scars from Afghanistan that will be there for life. I grew tired of being over there and decided not to re-enlist. My brother, Carter, called to see if I would be interested in a partnership with him and my other brothers. I jumped in with both feet and never looked back."

"That is great that you can work with your brothers and get along. I don't have any siblings, so having a big family sounds terrific to me."

"It is great but can sometimes be trying. My brothers and I can be very bullheaded at times. I am excited to become an uncle. Carter and Lillie will be having a baby soon."

"That is awesome."

"I think it will be pretty cool. I hope Carter and Lillie have a girl since our family is all men except Mom."

"Wow, I bet your mother has to be a strong woman raising four boys."

"Yes, she is and wonderful mother also."

Nikki's phone buzzed. She grabbed her phone from her purse and read the text. Nikki sighed and then glanced at Chase.

"I hate to do this to you, but I have a delivery," Nikki said regretfully. Chance waved his hand in dismissal.

"I understand; got to work to make money." Chance replied, standing up and pushing the chair back. Nikki did the same. " I would really like to see you again if possible." Chance stated as they walked back to his car.

"I would like that, Chance. I really had a wonderful time with you." Nikki replied, climbing inside his car.

"Would you like to get together on Sunday?"

"I would love to."

"Great, it is a date," Chance smiled, pulling into her apartment complex. Chance reached over, grabbing her hand into his. " I will pick you up around 12:00."

"Sounds good. Thank you, Chance, for the wonderful time today and last night especially." Nikki said, smiling.

"I will repeat last night anytime you want." Chance stated, then reached out, cupping the back of her head and pulling her towards him. His lips captured hers in a scorching kiss. Their tongues tangled and twisted together. The chance finally let loose of her lips. Nikki smiled at him with swollen lips.

"See you later, handsome," Nikki said, opening the car door and climbing out. Chance smiled, giving her a small wave as he pulled out of the parking lot. Nikki turned and waved.

Chapter 6

Saturday morning, Chance packed a picnic basket for Nikki and himself. He put together a fruit bowl and ham with cheese sandwiches. Chance grabbed several bottles of water, stuffing them into a cool pack. Everything had to fit into his backpack since they would be on mountain bikes.

Chance was excited about today since he had not seen Nikki in a week. Plus, he hadn't been able to ride his bike in a while, being busy at work installing security systems. Chance double-checked his backpack to ensure he had everything, food, water, and a first aid kit. Once satisfied, Chance loaded up the mountain bike in the back of the truck. He climbed into his truck heading to Nikki's place.

Chance parked his truck and climbed out as Nikki came out the front door of her apartment. She gave him a huge smile.

"Hey, handsome."

"Are you ready to work those sexy legs of yours?"

"Hell, yes, I am excited to start riding. My bike is in the garage."

Chance strolled towards her, following her to the garage. Nikki opened the garage door. She pointed to the corner where her bike was located.

"My bike is right over there."

"I will get it loaded up."

"Great, I am going to get my backpack."

Chance loaded up her bike while she ran into the house to get her pack. Nikki grabbed her backpack and locked the house. She walked towards him with spring in her step. Chance grabbed hold o her hand and pulled her into his arms. He bent his head down, capturing her lips in a toe-curling kiss. Nikki giggled and smiled up at him.

"Well, I like that hello."

"I missed you. I haven't seen you in a week. By the way, I love the biker outfit you got going on."

Nikki laughed and turned in a circle for him. She had on a hot pink cropped tank top that molded to her large breasts and showed off her toned, bare stomach. The shorts were black and molded to her like a second skin.

"Glad you like it. I definitely like riding shorts on you." Nikki licked her lips and winked at him, staring at the front of his shorts. Chance laughed, shaking his head. He really liked Nikki a lot. She was not scared to voice her opinion.

"Woman, you keep looking at me like that. We might have to cancel the ride."

"No, I will behave; come on, let's go. I am really excited to ride." Nikki opened the passenger door. Chance slapped her on the ass.

"Get on up in my truck before I change my mind."

Nikki giggled, climbing up into the truck. Chance closed her door and walked to the driver's side, climbing inside.

"You have everything you need before I pull out?"

"Um...yep. I packed sunscreen, riding gear, sunglasses, condoms, and water." Nikki giggled.

"I packed lunch and condoms." Chance wiggled his eyebrows at her smiling.

"Well, we are on the same wavelength then."

"Yes, we are." Chance laughed.

Chance drove about ten miles before parking his truck at the rail trail. They climbed out and unloaded the bikes. They both put on their riding gear. After strapping on the helmets, they climbed onto their bikes.

"Have you ever ridden on this trail, Nik?"

"No, I haven't been able to ride for a while."

"Today is your lucky day. This trail will give you a serious workout. It has a lot of uphill riding."

"I just hope I can keep up with you."

"Just yell if you need to rest, and we will stop. I plan on stopping at the little lake and going swimming."

"Shit, you didn't tell me about swimming. I didn't bring a suit."

"Neither did I." Chance laughed, wiggling his eyebrows at her suggestively.

"Wait, are you talking about swimming in the nude?"

"Hell yeah."

"Let's hurry. I feel like a swim."

"Now you are talking."

Chance and Nikki hopped on their bikes and started riding. Nikki followed behind Chance, enjoying the view in front of her. She about fell off her bike, watching his muscles flex as he moved on the bike. Everything on him rippled nicely.

It didn't take long to work up a sweat riding bikes. The weather was perfect, full sun and warm at 80'. There wasn't a cloud in the bright blue sky with a warm, slight breeze blowing.

After a half hour of pedaling uphill, they stopped for a quick drink of water. They both had sweat covering their bodies.

"How are you doing, Nik?" Chance asked, wiping sweat from his forehead. Nikki was doing the same and smiled at him.

"Definitely a workout, but I love the burn in my muscles."

"So, are you ready to move again?"

"Let's go; I can't wait to see you swim naked."

Chance laughed and climbed back on his bike. He loved riding on the bike trails. The woods were quiet and beautiful. The tree's canopy and the sun were giving them shade. He loved listening to the sounds of the animals scurrying about and birds singing.

Chance glanced over his shoulder to check on Niki. She was doing great keeping up with him. She was damn sexy, with her tanned skin glistening in the sun. She looked a little flushed from sweating. She would be able to cool down soon.

The lake was just around the next bend. Chance was surprised they hadn't run into any other bikers. In a way, he was glad because he would get her to go skinny dip with him. Half an hour later, the bend rounded, and the lake was sparkling in the sun.

"Oh my god, this is a beautiful spot," Nikki said, stopping on her bike.

"It is my favorite spot."

They both climbed off their bike. Nikki's legs felt a little rubbery. Her body was drenched in sweat. She looked at the water and smiled. The water looked very refreshing and cool. Chance grinned at the look of longing on her face.

"The water looks nice and cool for an overheated body, doesn't it?" Chance said, smiling.

"Yes, it does."

"I don't know about you, but I will take advantage of it before I eat lunch." Chance grinned at her taking off his biking gear. Nikki looked around to see if there were any other bikers around. She didn't hear or see anyone around.

She looked back towards Chance. Her eyes widened in shock, seeing him pulling his clothes off. Chance pulled his shirt off, tossing it on his bike. Next, he started removing his sock and tennis shoes.

"Oh my god, Chance! Are you really going skinny dipping?"

"Hell yes, why not? The water looks inviting and cool."

"But what if someone comes along and sees you naked."

"I plan on being in the deep end or at least enough to cover my bare ass."

"Seriously, you really are going in naked?"

"Yes, you are coming?" Chance dropped his shorts, laughing at Nikki's surprised look. He turned and ran full speed into the water, diving in. Nikki stood still with her mouth open in disbelief. She couldn't believe Chance had just dropped his shorts without care.

Nikki spread out the blanket on the ground for their lunch. She looked out towards the water. Nikki hadn't seen Chance come up from the water yet. She raised her hand to her forehead, shielding her eyes from the sun, looking for him. Nikki breathed a sigh of relief; she didn't realize she had been holding seeing his head pop up out of the water. Chance grinned at her shaking the water from his hair.

"Come on, Nik, the water feels amazing!" Chance yelled and moved closer to the shore. He stood up, water running down his bronzed chest. The water line was at his waist. Nikki just stared at him with appreciation. Damn, Chance was one sexy man.

"Come on, Nik, I am lonely out here."

"I don't have a swimming suit."

"Just leave your bra and panties on, then."

"I can't. I am not wearing any."

"You are commando under your riding suit?"

"Yes."

"Damn, woman. the water is cool, and you still can get me hard." Chance groaned. Nikki laughed. He gave her some hinder finger. She shook her head, no giggling.

"Come on, one will see you. We didn't run into anyone on the trail." Chance pleaded.

Nikki laughed harder at his pleading voice. She looked around again, not seeing or hearing any other bikers. Nikki sat down and pulled off her socks and tennis shoes. She moved closer to the water, putting her feet into the water.

"No guts, no glory, babe." Chance yelled, watching her.

"Are you bullying me?"

"Hell yes, come on in, chicken shit."

"You are an ass.'

"At least I am not a scaredy cat, chicken shit." Chance yelled. Nikki busted up laughing at his childish ribbing.

"Seriously, scaredy cat, chicken shit."

"Yep, sissy, Nancy boy, wimp, and all-time favorite pussy girl."

"You arrogant ass!" Nikki yelled back, pulling her clothes off and throwing them on the ground.

" I am coming in to drown your arrogant ass!"

Chance laughed loudly, watching her strip. He wasn't sure if she was really pissed off or if she was acting. He never saw a woman tear off her clothes that fast. She was stalking him with an angry, determined face.

His cock hardened more, seeing the angry look on her face and bouncing tits. Plus, she was absolutely gorgeous naked, and the water splashed up on her tanned skin.

"Um...Nik, I think I hear some bikers coming!" Chance yelled.

"What? Seriously?"

"Someone is coming down the trail."

"Oh my god!' Nikki drove into the water to cover herself up. She surfaced a few feet from him. She heard Chance laughing loudly as she emerged. Her heart was racing, looking over her should to see the intruders. She didn't see anyone.

"Where are they?" Nikki asked, looking around for the bikers. Chance grinned and shrugged his shoulders.

"I guess I was mistaken." Chance laughed.

"You ass!" Nikki yelled, splashing water at him. Chance laughed harder and splashed her back.

"Oh, you!" Nikki clamped her hands together, turning in a circle, hands making a splashing wave in the water.

Chance grinned and did the same thing. They both were laughing and acting like kids splashing each other. They hadn't even noticed they were being watched by another couple sitting on the water's edge.

"Hey, how's the water?" The man yelled out to them.

Both Nikki and Chance were startled by the male voice. Nikki's eyes were wide as she ducked into the water, covering her bare breasts.

"Oh my god, shit!' She moved out to the deeper water. Chance laughed. She slapped him as she passed by him. Chance could see the flush of embarrassment on her face.

"The water is great." Chance yelled back to the man and woman on the shore.

"Don't worry, we are not coming in. We noticed the clothes on the shore. We don't want to interrupt an intimate scene." The man stated, waving his hand at Chance.

"Thanks, it is appreciated." Chance yelled back.

"Have fun." The man said as they climbed back on their bikes and left. Chance laughed and waved at the couple. He turned around and didn't see Nikki.

"Nikki?" Chance said, looking for her. She didn't answer. Chance felt his heart beat faster, not knowing if Nikki knew how to swim.

"Nikki?" Chance yelled louder and quickly looked around again, not seeing her or the water moving. His heart raises up another notch.

"Nikki?" Chance yelled even louder and then heard a giggle. He quickly turned in circles, still not seeing her. he finally spotted a clump of trees to the right. He barely noticed the flash of tan skin tucked in the overhang of the tree branches hanging down.

"Nikki, where the hell are you, babe? You scaring me?" Chance heard the soft snicker again. He slowly made his way closer to her, acting like he hadn't seen her.

"Babe, you are really scaring me, Nik." Chance quickly and quietly dove under the water, swimming over to her. Nikki tried hard not to giggle out loud. She saw Chance coming towards her. She put her hand over her mouth.

Chance could see Nikki in front of him. He reached out and grabbed her legs. Nikki looked around, not seeing Chance. Her heart picked up speed looking for him.

All at once, she screamed at the feel of something on her leg pulling her under the water. Chance pulled her under the water with him. Nikki struggled against him, kicking. He let go of her struggling body and surfaced.

Nikki surfaced at the same time he did, choking and spewing out water from her mouth. Chance came up and pulled her into his arms. Nikki slapped her hands on his chest.

"Nikki, are you alright?" Chance asked, concerned, hearing her coughing.

"You asshole, you almost made me drown," Nikki said, coughing.

Chance wrapped his arms around her waist, pulling her close to his body and kissing the back of her head.

"Nik, I am sorry."

"You should be."

"I really am sorry." Chance said sincerely. Nikki turned around, wrapping her arms around his neck.

"Prove it," Nikki whispered.

Chance grinned and captured her cold lips. His tongue slid across her bottom lips, tasting the cold water on them. She opened her lips for him to slide his tongue inside. Their tongues tangled together in a passionate kiss. Chance felt her hard nipples press against his chest.

His hands slipped down to her bare ass, pulling up. Nikki raised her legs up and around his waist. She felt his hard erection against her stomach between them. Chance sucked and nibbled on her tongue. She moaned in his mouth, feeling the heat move to her center. Chande pulled his mouth from her and smiled.

"Shall we take this party to the shore?"

"Chance, what if someone else comes along?"

"Then, they will get an eye full."

"Are you serious?"

"Hell yes, I am hard as a rock, Nik. I want you."

"Chance, I..."

"Shush, doesn't it add to the excitement of getting caught.

Nikki looked at him, grinning from ear to ear. Her heart beat faster at the thought of his comment about being caught. She felt like a teenager making out on the couch, hoping not to get caught by her parents.

"Damn, I think you are right. My heart is racing just thinking about it."

Chance laughed and pushed her higher up on his hips. Nikki clung tighter as he walked through the water toward the shore. They both were naked on the day they were born. Nikki looked over her shoulder to see if anyone was watching them coming out of the water.

"Chance, you can put me down. I am probably getting heavy."

"Hell no, you weigh no more than a fly."

"Yeah, right, a horsefly is probably closer."

"Hell, I think my brother's dog, Oliver is heavier than you."

"Such a smooth talker you are."

"I will show you; I have a smooth tongue in just a few minutes." Chance said, grinning.

"Promises promises."

"Oh, I promise, alright. I will have you squirming under my tongue in two seconds flat." Chance bent down, plopping her down onto the blanket. He instantly dove between her legs and buried his face in her hot center. He grabbed her legs, setting them on his shoulders. He went down on her like a starved man, licking her wet folds with his flattened tongue.

Nikki's hips jerked at the instant arousal. Her body heated up a few degrees. His tongue lapped at her core like he was licking ice cream, sliding up and down. Nikki reached out, fishing his wet hair in her fingers.

Chance slid a finger inside her wet opening, moving it in and out. He heard her moan in desire. His lips latched on her swollen clit, sucking hard. His tongue circled the sensitive nub.

"Oh shit, Chance!" Nikki moaned as her hips jerked with the sensations moving through her body. Chance sucked and nipped her swollen clit whiling, moving fucking her with his finger moving in and out of her. He slid a second finger inside her slick opening. He felt her walls clench tightly around them, dragging them deeper inside her channel.

"Oh god, Chance!' Nikki moaned. Her hips began moving with the rhythm of his fingers. Her breathing grew heavy with her arousal. Her fingernails dug into his scalp. Chance pulled his fingers out of her and replaced them with his tongue, again lapping her cream. He reached up, pinched, and rolled her sensitive clit between his fingers.

"Oh yes, yes!" Nikki yelled as she went over the edge, climaxing. Chance continued to tongue fuck her. Nikki's body trembled, head moving back and forth as her fingers dug into his scalp. He slowed his rhythm down, gently bringing her back down.

Nikki started trying to wiggle away from him. Her body was ultra-sensitive from her orgasm. Chance pulled his mouth from her pussy and slid up her body. He rested his head on her breasts, looking up at her grinning.

"See, I keep my promised,"

"Yes, you did, and it was wonderful."

"That is great because I am nowhere near done with you."

NO?"

"Oh, hell no. I haven't even played with these magnificent tits yet."

Nikki laughed as Chance buried his face between her breasts. His hands came up to cup and mold them. Chance licked and sucked on every inch of her breasts, leaving nothing untouched. Her nipples stood out hard, erect, and sensitive.

Nikki felt her core throb and heat up again. Her skin tingled and flushed. His lips moved over her hard nipple, sucking it into his hot mouth. She moaned and gasped out at the feel of the sharp nip. The sensation edged on pain but turned to pleasure as the heat moved through her. Chance let go and moved to the other nipple doing the same thing.

Nikki gasped out loudly as a mini orgasm rippled through her. Her back arched, getting closer to him. Her hand pulled his hair in a tight grip.

"Damn," Chance said, letting loose of her nipple and raising his head, looking up at her pleasure-filled face. He smiled at her with a wicked grin.

"Damn, I love your tits."

"O my god, you just give me another orgasm with your wicked mouth."

"Good, I am not done yet, darling."

"No?"

"Not even close." Chance ground his hips against her. Nikki felt his hard erection pressing against her pelvis. He bent his head down, capturing her mouth in a toe-curling, passionate kiss. Nikki wrapped her arms around his neck. Chance deepened the kiss.

Nikki's heart rate ramped up a notch. She wrapped her legs around his waist, tilting her hips up to get closer to his hardness. Chance reached between their bodies, grabbing hold of his cock. He positioned it at her wet opening. He pumped his hips gently, entering her.

Nikki gasped as he pushed all the way inside of her. He stretched and filled her deliciously. She moaned her pleasure in his mouth. Chance stayed still for a few minutes giving her time to adjust to him. He slowly started moving in and out of her slick opening, loving the feel of her heat and tightness.

Nikki pulled her mouth from his. Her tongue slid up the side of his neck to ear, biting the lobe. Nikki's hand moved the body to his ass, caressing and squeezing the firm globes. Chance shivered and groaned.

Their bodies started moving together as the excitement increased. Chance rose up on his knees and pulled her hips up. At this angle, he could sink into her deeper. Grabbing her hips, he started pumping inside her deeper and harder. He watched her large breast jiggle up and down. Her face was flushed and beautiful, eyes filled with desire, biting her bottom lip.

Chance reached down and started rubbing her swollen clit. He watched her bite her bottom lip harder as her body trembled underneath him. Her head rolled side to side. He felt her walls clench his cock tighter. He knew she was on the edge.

"Are you ready to cum, Nik?"

"Oh god, yes!" Chance snickered at her answer and rubbed her clit harder.

"How close?"

"Very close," Nikki moaned out. Chance pinched her clit. Her wall clenched his cock hard. he pulled almost out of her channel and then slammed back in hard and deep.

"Oh yes, please!"

"Are you going to cum for me?"

"Yes, Yes!" Nikki panted out. Chance almost pulled out and slammed into her again, pinching her clit simultaneously. Her walls convulsed around his cock as she went over the edge.

"Chance, right there. Yes!" Nikki screamed. Chance felt the prickling sensation run down his spine straight to his balls. His cock swelled and jerked inside of her as his orgasm hit.

"Fuck!" Chance growled. Loudly as he exploded inside her. Their hips moved frantically as their orgasm mingled together. They both were breathing heavily. Chance felt the tension release from his body as he emptied himself inside her.

Chance collapsed onto her. Nikki welcomed his weight loving the feel of his body on her. She wrapped her arms around him. Chance nuzzled the side of her neck.

"God, it was awesome." Nikki giggled, and his lips nibbled on her sensitive spot.

"Yes, it was."

"Damn, I need a nap now. You tired me out, woman."

"We need to get dressed first before someone sees us."

"I like being naked with you in the sunshine and woods."

"So do I, but we are out in the open."

"I don't care; I am comfortable right here."

"Chance?" Nikki said and started to wiggle under him. She was ready to get dressed before someone else came along, catching them naked.

"Fine, poor sport. I am going to take a quick swim first." Chance said, rolling off her and standing up. He headed to the water. Nikki watched him stroll to the water and dive in. She found her clothes and began to dress. She sat down, grabbed the basket, and pulled out their lunch.

She swallowed hard, watching Chance walk towards her naked with water running off his tan, muscular body. She couldn't believe how comfortable he was naked outside. He grinned at her.

"Stop staring, or you be naked again."

"I couldn't help myself. You look like a Greek god, all naked and gorgeous."

Chance laughed and grabbed his clothes. While he got dressed, she finished setting out their lunch. After getting dressed, Chance sat down on the blanket and started eating. They eat quietly, listening to the sounds of the woods around them.

"I love it out here, the quiet and the fresh smell."

"I do, too; I bike ride on these trials at least once a week."

"I need to make more time for myself, but my business seems to be getting busier.'

"Nik, that is a good thing, but you do need to take one day for yourself."

"You are right. All business and no play is not good."

"Are you ready to hit the trail back?"

"Yes, I am ready."

They packed away the leftover food and picked up the blanket. They climbed on their bikes and headed the two hours back to the truck. They were tired by the time they made it to the truck. Chance loaded up the bikes. Nikki sat down on the edge of the fence, smiling.

"That was great. My body is feeling it now; muscles are getting tight." Nikki said.

"You used muscles that haven't been used in a while."

"I am going to be sore tomorrow for sure."

"You will need to soak in a hot bath later or get a massage."

"Um...now that sounds like heaven."

"I do know a great massager."

"You do? What is their name?"

"Chance Black."

"Really, I know a Chance also. A chance I would like to take."

"This Chance would also like to take a chance with a certain woman named Nikki Curtis."

"I like that we think alike." Nikki stood up and walked over to Chance, wrapping her arms around his neck. Chance pulled her up tight against his hot, sweating body bending his head and capturing her lips in a scorching kiss. Nikki melted against him as his tongue mated with hers, tangling and twisting. They pulled apart when they heard voices coming towards them from the trail. The couple they had seen earlier came out from the trail. They waved at each other as they bypassed. Nikki and Chance laughed.

Chance opened the truck door for Nikki. She climbed up inside the truck, closing the door. Chance climbed into the driver's seat and pulled out of the parking lot. He headed back to Nikki's apartment.

Once at Nikki's apartment, Chance unloaded her bike from his truck. He wheeled the bike into the garage, putting it away. Nikki watched him smiling. Chance turned, catching her and watching him.

"Do I have dirt on my ass?"

"No, you have a sexy toned ass."

"Why are you staring at me, then?"

"Because you are one sexy, hot man and pleasant on the eyes."

"I bet you say that all the men."

"Wrong! You are the best-looking one I have seen in a long time."

"Not true. I saw you drooling over my brother, Chase, the other day."

"What! Well, he is kind of hot in a Paul Walker sort of way." Nikki stated, grinning. Chance reached over, slapping her hard on the ass. Nikki gasped out loud and then laughed.

"What was that for?"

"For noticing my brother's good looks."

"Noticed, but you are my type, strong, broad shoulders, tall with the perfect abs and v-shape."

"Is that so?" Chance said, grabbing her by the waist and pulling her up nice and tight to his hard body. Nikki looked up at his smiling, then ran her tongue over her bottom lip, watching Chance's eyes track her tongue. Nikki's tongue left a wet trail on her bottom lips.

Chance couldn't resist bending his head and running his tongue over her bottom lip. Nikki's tongue came out to meet his, opening her mouth. Chance captured hers in a heated, passionate kiss. They tasted each other in hunger, tongues twisting and mating. When they finally pulled apart, both were aroused and breathless. They stared at each with hunger.

"Is that message still available, Mr. Black?" Nikki asked breathlessly.

"Hell, yes!" Chance replied.

"Great," Nikki said, grabbing his hand and pulling him towards the side apartment door. Nikki closed the garage door and then dragged Chance through the door straight to her bedroom. They devoured each again, standing by the bed. They pulled apart again breathlessly.

"Get undressed." Chance stated firmly. Nikki nodded her head.

"You too!" Nikki said, pulling off her biker top. Chance's eyes darkened, watching her large breasts bounce after being released from her top.

"Damn, I love your tits." Chance state. Nikki laughed, pulling off her bike shorts and standing before him naked. Chance stared at her openly without touching her.

"Lay on our stomachs on the bed." Chance stated.

Nikki climbed on the bed; she turned so her head was at the edge of the bed. She looked up at Chance with a grin.

"Take your shorts off. I want to suck your cock as you massage me." Nikki said seductively, licking her bottom lips. Chance laughed, pulling off his t-shirt. Nikki watched him undress, feeling the dampness between her legs. Chance grabbed his cock, stroking himself several times, watching Nikki's eyes widen in hunger. He chuckled, then moved slowly to her, standing before the bed.

"Is this what you want, babe?" Chance whispered, holding his cock.

"God, I love the size of you," Nikki reached out, grabbing his hard-on. Chance moved closer as Nikki stroked his cock a few times. Chance bent over so he could massage her shoulders and back.

Nikki swirled her hot wet tongue around his mushroom head, lapping the pre-cum from the slit. Chance moaned at the feel of her wet tongue licking him. Chance's hands kneaded the knots out of her shoulders and back. Nikki opened her mouth wider, going down on him. Chance moved his hips slowly to the movement of her mouth sliding up and down his stiff shaft. Nikki moaned around his cock, sending vibrations straight to his balls.

"Damn, your mouth feels like heaven." Chance moaned in pleasure, pumping his hips a little faster as the need grew stronger. Chance ran his hands up and down her back, massaging her tight muscles. Nikki sucked his cock harder, making another groan slip from his lips.

"Babe, I am close to coming." Chance growled, feeling the tingling sensation start in his spine. Nikki hummed around his cock, sending the sensation straight to his balls. Chance's cock jerked inside her mouth, growing thicker with his arousal.

"Nik, babe, I want to cum inside you, not your mouth." Chance growled, stepping back and pulling his cock from her heavenly mouth. His cock made a pop sound sliding out from her mouth. Nikki wiped her mouth, smiling.

Nikki turned over, getting up on her hands and knees before him. She looked over her shoulder, grinning, then wiggled her ass at him.

"Fuck, you are so fucking sexy. I can see you are wet for me."

"I am so ready for you," Nikki whispered.

Chance grabbed a condom and quickly rolled it on, then moved up the bed on his knees behind her wide-spread legs. He reached up, caressing her ass, then positioned his cock at her slick opening. Chance thrust his hips, entering inside her in one push. A couple more pumps of his hips, and he was deep inside her hot channel. They both moaned with the feeling of being joined. Chance stayed still for a couple of seconds before moving.

"Please, Chance," Nikki panted, pushing back against him. Chance thrust his hips and buried his balls deep inside her.

"Babe, you want slow and easy or hard and fast?" Chance growled out.

"Hard and fast, Chance. I ready to cum," Nikki groaned.

"No coming." Chance growled out.

"Please!"

"No, not yet," Chance stated, smiling, then pounding his cock hard and fast like she had begged. He pumped into her with short hard thrusts of his hips. His ball banged against her. Chance reached down, rubbing her swollen clit in firm circles.

"Chance!" Nikki screamed as her walls clenched his cock tightly. Nikki's body tingled all over as her orgasm built inside her. Her pussy pulsated around his cock, taking him deep inside her.

"Fuck Nik!" Chance panted out, feeling her pussy flutter around his cock.

"Coming!" Nikki moaned, going over the edge. Her come coated his cock, making him slip in and out of her with slurping noises. Chance felt his balls draw up, and the tingling sensation grew stronger inside him. He couldn't hold back any longer. Chance exploded inside her slick hot channel. Chance growled loudly as he pounded into her until he was empty. Sweat rolled down his spine, breath coming out heavily when he laid his head on her back spent.

"Fuck!" Chance panted out. Nikki giggled, falling flat on the bed and taking Chance with her. They played tangled up for a few minutes until Chance caught his breath. He knew he was heavy and rolled off Nikki onto his back.

Nikki looked over at him, smiling. Chance smiled back.

"Damn, we are explosive together."

"I know. It is fucking terrific." Chance said, pulling off the used condom and tossing it into the trash beside the bed. Nikki snuggled up to his side, resting her head on his shoulder. Chance's hand caressed her back. He looked over at the clock. It read 3:00p.m. He didn't want to move but had to.

"Damn, I don't want to get up." Chance said.

"Then don't."

"I have to. I promised to help my dad today."

"Well, then, you better get up. I don't want your dad to be pissed at me for you breaking a promise to him." Nikki said, rolling away from him. Chance slapped her on the ass.

"God, I love your sass." Chance laughed.

"Not many people do, so I am glad." Nikki grabbed a bathrobe slipping it over her naked body. Chance slipped off the bed and began getting dressed. He walked over to Nikki and pushed the lapel apart on her robe, exposing her large breasts to his eyes. Chance fondled them. His thumbs circled her nipples until they were hard nubs. He bent his head, lifting them to his waiting mouth, latching on to the nipple, sucking on it hard. Nikki gasped out, then moaned.

"Chance," Nikki moaned loudly.

"I love your tits." Chance growled, nipping her nipple.

"Stop," Nikki moaned. Chance let go of her nipple, making a popping noise. He captured her lips in a passionate kiss. After fully tasting every inch of her mouth, he let loose of her.

"I need to go before I take you back to bed." Chance whispered against her lips. Nikki nodded her head, stepping back from him. Chance laughed.

"Go," Nikki said, pointing to the door.

"See you later. Thanks, Nik; I had a great time today," Chance said, smiling.

"Me too, now go. Your dad is waiting," Nikki said, smiling. Chance turned quickly back to her, kissed her, then walked to the front door.

"Bye, Nik," Chance said, walking out the front door. Nikki smiled, watching him leave her apartment. She was grateful to Justin and Dean for introducing her to Chance. She thought maybe she had finally found the right person who would fit into her life.

Chapter 7

On Thursday, Nikki was preparing her plane to fly Chase Black to Utah to meet his girlfriend, Jaci Hurst. She had done her pre-flight check before he arrived so everything would be ready. Nikki spotted a black truck drive up to the warehouse. She recognized the truck as Chance's.

Chance and Chase climbed out of the truck. Damn, they were two sexy men coming toward her. Chance smiled and walked towards Nikki. Chase walked to the back of the truck to grab his duffel bag. Chance walked up to Nikki and wrapped his arms around her.

"Hello, you sexy, hot woman." Chance said, smiling reaching out and pulling her into his arms.

"I could say the same about you, handsome," Nikki said. Chance laughed and then captured her mouth in a toe-curling kiss. They pulled apart when Chase cleared his throat behind them. They both laughed at his interruption.

"Chase, in two hours, you will be locking lips with Jaci," Chance smiled and punched Chase in the arm.

"Damn right, I will. Nikki, you have got yourself a beautiful plane. It had to cost a pretty little penny."

"Yes, it did. I am still paying for it. You can put your luggage on the plane. The plane is already for takeoff. I already did my pre-flight check."

Chase walked over to the stairs and walked up into the plane. He disappeared inside the plane with his luggage.

"Chance, would you like to come with us? It will take about five hours to fly there and back." Nikki said.

"Let me call Carter first to see if he can spare me," Chance replied, smiling, and pulled his cell phone out of his pocket.

"Hello, Chance. What's up?" Carter asked.

"Is there anything important that needs to down today at work?" Chance asked.

"Nope, it is pretty quiet in the office today. Why?"

"Nikki is flying Chase to Utah to meet up with Jaci, and I thought about riding along."

"Sounds like fun."

"So, it that a yes, Chance, I don't need you today."

"That would be a yes. Have a great time."

"Thanks, Carter."

"By the way, you don't have to ask for my permission. Just tell me you won't be coming in."

"Noted."

"See you later."

"Later, Carter." Chance walked over to where Nikki was standing and smiled.

"You have a co-pilot."

"Great, let's board then," Nikki waved her hand towards the plane, smiling.

They walked up the stairs to the plane. Chance was impressed with the inside of the aircraft. There were two tan leather seats, a small fridge, and a bathroom. Along the wall was a brown leather bench couch.

Chance could tell the plane wasn't very old, maybe five years old at the most. Everything still looked pretty new inside the plane. Chace was sitting in one of the chairs, smiling at them.

"Chase, I am riding along with the two of you." Chance smiled.

"Great to have you aboard, brother." Chase laughed.

Nikki was excited that Chance was riding along. He took a seat in the co-pilot spot. Chance put on the headphones and listened to her as she did her flight plans with the tower. Chance realized how much he missed flying sitting in the co-pilot seat.

It had been a couple of years since he had been in a pilot's seat. Listening to Nikki, he knew he hadn't forgotten a thing. It was like riding a bike; once you learn, you never forget.

Nikki got the okay to take off. She revved the engines up, and the plane started moving. Nikki had to turn the plane around. Once she had the plane in position for takeoff. Nikki taxied the plane down the runway the tower wanted her to use. She waited for the tower to tell her; she could take off.

"This is my favorite part. Having all this power and speed beneath my ass and hand," Nikki said excitedly. Chance laughed.

Nikki received the okay to go. She revved the engine and started moving down the runway faster as it taxied. Chance watched her hand on the throttle, pushing it further down as the plane moved faster. All at once, Chance was transported back to Afghanistan.

Chance was flying the medical helicopter in the middle of the war zone. He was called in to pick up some injured men. As he passed the helicopter, he saw gunfire and bombs being exchanged below them. He was flying into dangerous territory. Chance, Justin, and Dean had to keep their eyes open for trouble. They both were filled with adrenaline rushes and very alert.

Chance and Justin had been told the ordinances of where to pick up the injured men. Twelve men down needed to be transported back to the hospital. Chance and Justin were in heavy action territory and needed to keep aware of the fire exchange around them. Chance found the touchdown spot. So far, everything has been going smoothly.

Chance landed the helicopter smoothly. Justin and Dean picked up the first six injured men and loaded them into the helicopter with no problems. As soon as the wounded men were secure, Chance took off, flying the men back to the infirmary. They unloaded the men then Chance had to return for the other six injured men. He hoped this trip would go just as smoothly as the first.

When returning for the other six men, Chance noticed more action below. The pickup spot was under heavy arterially action. Chance was not sure if he was going to be able to land. He kept looking for a safe place to land without taking any hits.

"Justin, I don't see a safe place to land. There is a lot of action down there." Chance stated.

"Fuck, I don't see a safe place either."

"I see them waving for us to land." Chance stated. "I hear them screaming to land."

"What do you think, Chance?" Justin asked.

"We have to get those men out. I am going to take the chance." Chance replied as he slowly began to take the chipper down. Chance was almost ready to land the chopper when he felt a hot, burning pain in his left arm. He looked down at his arm. His shirt sleeve was turning red.

"Fuck, I have been hit," Chance yelled in pain.

"What the fuck!" Justin yelled back, looking over at Chance.

Chance had the urge to let loose of the controls to grab his bleeding arm but kept a firm grip on the controls. He held the chopper steady as it continued to move closer to the landing place.

"Where have you been hit, Chance?" Justin asked, concerned.

"In the fucking arm," Chance yelled over all the noise. He landed the plane on the ground.

"Are you alright?" Justin asked. Chance nodded his head.

"Don't worry about me. The other men need your help more than I do." Chance stated. Justin nodded, then climbed out of the chopper to help load the other six men. They got the men loaded.

Chance started to raise the chopper after all the men had been loaded. Then all at once, Chance felt something slam into his shoulder, leaving a burning path like his arm. This one knocked the wind out of him. Chance gasped out in tremendous pain.

"Fuck," Chance yelled out, letting go of the controls.

His hand instantly went to his left shoulder. Chance felt the warm sticky feeling of blood oozing between his fingers. He looked down, and his hand was covered in blood. The chopper started to wave side to side and then spin in a circle. Chance looked over at Justin. Justin could see the fear on Chance's face and then knew something was wrong.

"Holy shit, Chance," Justin yelled as the chopper started turning in a circle. Justin quickly grabbed the controls to steady the helicopter. The chopper was close enough to the ground it landed a little rougher than usual. Justin looked over at Chance.

Chance was feeling lightheaded from the blood pooling out of him. The front of his shirt was now soaked with blood. Chance knew the bullet had hit a main artery because of all the blood pouring from him.

"Chance, how are you doing?" Justin yelled at him. Justin sounded so far away as Chance tried to stay coherent. Chance saw black spots behind his eyes and knew he was getting ready to pass out.

"Just....need...to...fly... I...can't." Chance replied, slurring his words and fighting the blackness. Chance slumped over the seat.

When Chance woke up, he was in the makeshift hospital. His left shoulder and arm were all bandaged up. He felt like he had been hit by a truck. The nurse came into the room.

"How are you feeling, Mr. Black," The nurse asked.

"Like I got hit by a truck," Chance replied.

"I am sure you do. Do you remember what happened to you?"

"Yes, I got shot in the arm and shoulder." Chance stated, looking at the bandages.

"Yes, you are correct. You are one lucky man. A few more centimeters to the left, you would not be here. The bullet almost hit your heart. It is going to take some time for that injury to heal."

"I guess I am fortunate then." Chance replied.

"You also lost a lot of blood. You will feel weak and tired until your body replenishes the blood supply. We had to give you a couple bags of blood

to stabilize you. Your comrade Justin had to do CPR on you. He got you stable enough when they brought you here."

"I remember blacking out."

"You went into cardiac arrest from the blood loss."

"I died.?" Chance said in shock. The nurse nodded her head. "Justin saved me?" Again, the nurse nodded her head.

"Jeezus!" Chance said with shock.

"As I said, you are one lucky man, Mr. Black," The nurse stated.

"Chance, are you okay? Chance!" Nikki asked with concern shaking his arm. Chance looked like he was in a trance. His face was pale, and his body was shaking.

"Chase, something is wrong with Chance!" Nikki yelled out to Chase. Chase hurried to the front of the plane. Chase shook Chance's arm. Chance's eyes were unfocused.

"Hey, Chance," Chase said, patting him on the face. Chance finally blinked his eyes and looked at Chase with confusion.

"What happened to you, bro?" Chase asked worriedly.

"Sorry, I had a flashback of being shot in Afghanistan."

"Yes, that does happen to all of us military crew," Chase stated.

"I haven't had one in a while. The flying must have triggered it with me being in the co-pilot seat." Chance said, embarrassed. Chase patted him on the shoulder, understanding. Chance was still embarrassed that he spaced out in front of Nikki. Chase went back to sit in his seat again. Chance glanced over at Nikki and saw her concern.

"You okay? You were out of it for a little while?" Nikki asked, concerned.

"Yes, sorry, I didn't mean to scare you."

"No need to be sorry, Chance."

"Man, I forgot how beautiful it is to fly," Chance said, looking out the window.

"I love it. It does get a little lonely up here by myself when I am making my deliveries."

"I am sure it does. Have you ever thought of hiring a co-pilot?"

"Are you interested?" Nikki glanced over at him smiling.

"It is something I could consider when I am not busy at work."

"Let me know. I definitely would consider a hot, sexy co-pilot." Nikki winked at him.

"You must be considering me, not Chance," Chase said, laughing. Chance punched Chase in the arm.

"You have your own woman."

"Yes, I do. Jaci is quite a handful. Nothing is ever dull when Jaci is around."

"At least you haven't been in the tabloids lately since giving her a public spanking," Chance chuckled.

"No, Jaci enjoys getting spanked too much now. Spanking isn't for bad behavior now, if you know what I mean," Chase said, wiggling his eyebrows. Chance and Nikki laughed.

"I think I like Jaci. I bet we would get along great," Nikki stated.

"Well, maybe, the next time you fly me to where she is, you can spend a couple of days with us. I would invite you this time, but I haven't seen her in a month. I plan to keep her in bed the next couple of days."

"Chase, your dog, too much information for us." Chance laughed.

"Hey, we are great together, besides there is never enough loving time for Jaci," Chase stated. Nikki was reading the accordance to the tower and not listening to Chance or Chase's conversation.

"You got your hands full with this one," Chase said, looking at Nikki.

"Yeah, I really like her even though I just met her." Chance said softly.

"Sometimes that doesn't matter; you just fit together immediately."

"Carter and Lillie did, even though she had to convince Carter of that."

"With Jaci, I had to see the other side of her. I didn't like the fouled-mouth rocker, but I was still attracted to her."

"Jaci definitely is a different person off-stage. She is two people, a bad girl and a sensual woman."

"I love the sensual part the most."

Nikki stopped talking in the headphones. She turned to Chance and Chase.

"We will be landing in about 20 minutes. So, buckle up, gentleman, and get ready to land. Thank you for picking Nikki's pleasure flight for your needs." Nikki giggled. Chance and Chase laughed.

Nikki received the okay to land the plane on the runway. She started to descend. Chance didn't realize he tensed up and held his breath. Nikki landed the plane smoothly. She looked over at Chance, smiling. Chance was pale and had a death grip on the dash panel. When the plane came to a complete stop, Chance finally let out a breath. He felt embarrassed by his reaction.

Chance slowly glanced over at Nikki to see if she noticed his reaction. She was busy checking the instrument panel. Chase was on his cell phone talking to Jaci. She was in the airport waiting for him to arrive. Chase grabbed his luggage.

"Am I all set to leave?" Chase asked anxiously.

"Yes, you are. We have to sit here for half an hour before leaving again." Nikki stated.

"Great, So I will see you on Sunday at 4:00 pm. Thank you so much, Nikki. I will see you later, Chance." Chase said as Nikki opened the exit door for him. The airport already had the stairs set up next to the plane.

"Have fun; tell Jaci hello for me." Chance said.

"Later," Chase waved, then walked down the stairs. Nikki pulled the door shut and locked it. She then walked back to the cockpit and sat down. Nikki put her headphones back on and informed the tower she was ready to leave again.

"Chance, you okay to take off again?" Nikki asked, concerned.

“Yes, I am fine.”

"Great, we are fifth in line for takeoff."

Nikki turned her attention to her instrument panel. She listened to the tower's instructions for the runway she needed. Chance also heard with the other headphones. He checked everything Nikki was doing. She was an excellent pilot. Nikki definitely knew what she was doing. She was, after all, an Air Force airwoman.

The plane started to move. Nikki moved in line for takeoff. After 15 minutes, she received the okay to go. Nikki began to move down the runway picking up speed. It didn't take long to be airborne again.

This time Chance didn't have any flashbacks. He was more relaxed this time. Chance listened on his headphones to the tower. Nikki looked over at him when the plane was flying altitude. Chance smiled at her. She smiled back, knowing he was okay this time.

“When do you fly out again?” Chance asked.

“Monday, I have delivery to Costa Rica. I will be gone about four days.”

“Do you have a lot of deliveries there?”

"Yes, one of our clients does a lot of business in Nicaragua and Costa Rica. He keeps me very busy also. My client's name is Hector Stamos."

Chance tensed hearing her client's name. He knew the name. The man was a millionaire. Hector Stamos was also under suspicion of trafficking drugs and women. He also rubbed elbows with a lot of influential people.

"I don't want to be rude, Nikki, but Hector Stamos has a lot of money and is very chummy with many influential people. Why would he have an independent pilot to deliver his good?"

"I deliver most of his goods to his two sons, Juan and Joseph," Nikki stated. Chance was still concerned about the deliveries.

"Juan and Joseph are great. The two of them have some awesome parties. Juan and Joseph have always treated me respectfully and are always happy to see me."

"Are the deliveries already prepacked when they come to you?"

"Chance, what is wrong? Why all the questions?" Nikki asked, concerned by his behavior.

"I am sorry. It really is none of my business." Chance said. Nikki looked over at him.

"Chance, something is bothering you. What is it?"

"Nikki, just be careful."

"I always am. I make damn good money by flying. I am known for being on time and dependent."

"Well, that is great. That is how a business should be run."

They landed in Dallas around 6:00 pm. Nikki put her plane in the warehouse she rented for it. They walked out to the parking lot.

"Thank you for letting tag along today, Nik," Chance said, pulling her into his arms. Nikki wrapped her arms around his neck.

"I am glad you came."

"I am sorry for the little episode. That has not happened in a long time. Flying must have triggered it."

"What was the flashback, Chance?"

"Of being shot. I don't know if Justin ever told you, but he saved my life that day."

"No, he has never said a thing."

"I didn't know until the nurse told me that Justin had to do CPR on me. I died, and Justin revived me."

"Wow, you were lucky, man."

"Yes, I was. I almost bled out. The bullet missed my heart, my centimeters."

"Shit! I am glad Justin saved your life; otherwise, you wouldn't be standing here with me."

"You are correct. I owe my life to Justin, but he will not hear of it. I tell him all the time thanks. Justin just waves his hand at me in dismissal."

"I love Justin and Dean. They were my closest friends in the Air Force."

"They are a couple of great guys."

"Yes, they are." Chance captured her lips in a passionate kiss. After a toe-curling kiss, they finally parted.

"I will see you later," Nikki said, letting her arms fall from his neck. She unlocked her car and then opened the door.

"Bye, babe," Chance said, walking to his truck. Nikki waved to him and climbed into her car. Chance climbed into his truck and watched her pull away. Chance pulled out onto the road and headed for home.

Chapter 8

Nikki was getting her plane ready for her delivery in Costa Rica. She was waiting for the shipment of goods to arrive. The shipment she would be delivering to the Stamos brothers.

The Stamos family was one of her biggest clients and paid her generously. Hector Stamos was the head of the household. Juan and Joseph were his sons. She did deliveries at least once a week for them. The money they paid her made the payment on her plane and covered the rest of her bills plus the leftover she put away for safekeeping.

Hector's guys finally arrived with the shipment of goods. Everything was packed up in boxes. They loaded the boxes into the plane for her. She knew she should actually be checking the shipment, but she was already running late.

Hector's right-hand man handed her an envelope. She knew there was $50,000.00 in cash in it. Nikki smiled at him and thanked him. Hector always paid her in cash. Every time she did a delivery, he paid her between $50,000.00 and $75,000.00.

Nikki knew what she was doing could be illegal. She never tampered with the boxes once they were loaded onto her plane. The less she knew about the shipment, the better. The money was too good to turn her back on.

Nikki did a couple of other deliveries for clients. She made a different amount of money than she did for Hector. The other jobs paid between $5,000 and $10,000. Those payments she recorded on her flight schedule books but not Hector's. She kept those payments off her books.

Nikki figured the shipments weren't illegal because she never got stopped by customs in Costa Rica. They checked her plane every time she landed but didn't check the load. Nikki would give them an envelope with the list of goods she was carrying. She knew it was wrong, but the money was too good to walk away from.

They would smile and sign the paperwork that they checked the shipment. Nikki figured they were getting paid not to open the load. Nikki knew the less she knew, the better if anything happened. Juan and Joseph would always be at the airport to meet her.

They would have a couple of men with them to unload the plane. They would then take her back to their house or hotel for a few days before she left again.

The shipment was set and ready to go. Nikki walked to her locker and put the envelope inside. She had enough money for her trip. She then locked it up and put the key in her purse.

Nikki walked over to the plane and climbed in. She had about a six-hour flight to Costa Rica. Nikki put on her headphones and told the tower she was ready to take off. They told her what runway was in the lineup. She would be in Costa Rich around 5:00 pm if everything went well. Nikki lined up the plane and got ready for takeoff.

After about twenty minutes, Nikki was given the okay to leave. She loved this part the best, speeding down the runway. Nikki revved the engine and took off down the runway. She wished Chance could have come with her.

They had been dating for about three weeks now. Nikki really liked him. They always had a great time together, and the sex was amazing. Chance could keep up with his sexual appetite. He was terrific at pleasuring her.

Nikki also loved his family. Lillie was a beautiful, sweet woman with a round pregnant belly. Her husband Carter was devoted to her. Chase and Jaci would be a lot of fun to hang out with. With Jaci being famous, they would have to be careful where they went, or Jaci would get mobbed by fans. Colin was the single brother. Nikki smiled, thinking of the fun she and Chance had the other night.

Chance and Nikki had gone out to eat, then to a movie. Afterward, they went back to Chance's house. They grabbed a bottle of wine and headed to Chance's hot tub.

"I don't have a bathing suit," Nikki said, smiling.

"No suits a loud." Chance said, taking off his shirt. He unbuttoned and unzipped his jeans. Chance gave Nikki a wicked smile. He then slowly slid his pants down and then his boxer briefs.

"Damn, you are one hot man, all hard and beefy," Nikki laughed.

"You keep looking at me with hunger in your eyes. I am going to have to feed you." Chance said seductively. Nikki laughed and licked her lips.

"I am going to eat you." Nikki purred.

"Damn, I am game."

Nikki pulled her shirt off. She unclasped her bra and slowly took it off. Nikki knew Chance liked her big breasts. She cupped her breast and watched Chance's eyes darken and glow with hunger.

"Damn, I love your tits." Chance stated. Nikki laughed.

Nikki unbuttoned and unzipped her jeans. She slowly wiggled out of them. Chance's eyes widened, looking at her heart-shaped thong. Nikki giggled.

"You like my heart?" Nikki asked seductively.

"Yes, I do like it very much." Chance moved closer to her.

Chance stood in front of her. His hands automatically went to her breasts, cupping and molding them. Chance ran his thumbs over her nipples. Nikki shivered at his touch. Chance's hands moved down her sides and then down to her ass.

Chance cupped and caressed her ass. He pulled her closer to him. Nikki felt his hard erection pressing against her. Then he started to rub his cock against her heart thong. Nikki moaned at the feel of his hard length grinding against her.

Chance picked her up and sat her on the edge of the hot tub. Nikki put her arms around his neck and pulled his head towards her. She captured his lips, sliding her tongue inside his mouth. Their tongues tangled and dueled in need.

Chance moved his body between her spread legs. He rubbed his cock up and down over her heart thong. Nikki's thong was becoming damp from his teasing and her need. His fingers rolled and pinched her nipples until they were hard nubs.

Chance pulled his mouth away from hers. His lips moved to her neck, running his tongue slowly down to her breasts. His hands pushed her heavy breasts up to meet his mouth and tongue. Chance's tongue swirled around the stiff peaks, sucking them into his mouth. He nibbled on the sweet nubs. Nikki moaned, running her hands through his hair.

"Damn, I love your big tits."

"I want you to slide your cock between them and titty fuck me," Nikki moaned, letting go of his head and sliding to the edge of the hot tub. Nikki then slipped off her thong and climbed into the hot tub. She sat on the bench, squeezing her breasts together and giving Chance a seductive smile.

"Come here, handsome, and fuck my tits," Nikki said, cupping her breast together.

"With pleasure." Chance growled, climbing into the hot tub. He stood in front of Nikki. She spread her legs so he could move closer to her. Nikki reached out and grabbed his cock. She bent her head and licked the mushroom head a few times.

Nikki positioned his stiff cock between her breasts. She cupped and pushed her breast around his cock. Chance smiled as he slid his cock up and down between her tightly held tits. Nikki bent her head and licked the head of his cock when he slid upwards.

"Shit, Nik, your tits feel great wrapped around my cock." Chance growled, sliding his cock faster between her breasts.

"Chance, I want you to come all over my tits." Nikki moaned, watching the head of his cock peek out of cupped breasts.

Nikki gripped his cock tighter between her breasts. She then moved her breasts up and down to massage his cock. Chance moaned in pleasure.

Chance's cock jerked, and he growled as he started to come. His cum shot between her breasts, making them slick.

Chance's cock slid faster as he emptied himself on her breasts. Nikki spread his cum all over her breasts, smiling, then licked her hands. Chance sat down next to her and gave her a huge smile.

"Stand up, baby. I want to taste your sweetness," Chance said seductively, licking his lips. Nikki stood up in front of him. She wasn't sure what he wanted.

"Stand on the bench and put one leg on the edge of the hot tub."

Nikki put her right leg on the hot tub above his shoulder. Now her pussy was even with his face. Chance pulled her to his mouth. Chance buried his face in her sex. He sucked her clit into his mouth. He ran his finger through her wet folds up and down. After spreading her moisture, he slips his finger inside her wet channel.

Chance moved his finger in and out of her slowly while his mouth sucked on her clit. Nikki moaned loudly at the feel of his finger inside her and his mouth teasing her. Her hips moved with the rhythm of his finger inside her. Nikki felt his other hand slide down her ass. She pushed against his hand. His finger probed her hole, making her shutter in need.

"Yes," Nikki moaned out.

Chance slowly and gently pushed his finger inside her ass. He waited a few seconds for her to get used to the invasion before moving it in and out. He moved both fingers in and out of her body. Nikki's walls started to clench his fingers in need. Chance gently bit her clit. Nikki's body trembled underneath him. His fingers became slick with her orgasm.

"Chance!"

"I got you, baby."

"Feels so good," Nikki moaned, trembling with her release.

Chance slowed his fingers down as her orgasm slowed down. He pulled his slick fingers out of her. He then licked the entire length of her pussy, lapping up the rest of her cream before releasing her. Nikki sat down next to him.

"What a glass of wine?" Chance asked.

"Sounds great," Nikki replied. Chance stood up and leaned over the edge of the hot tub. He opened the wine and poured them a glass. He handed her the glass of wine and sat down next to her.

"Damn, we are good together," Chance said, smiling.

"Yes, we are explosive."

"I like that, explosive together." Chance bent over and captured her mouth. He sucked the wine from her tongue and then pulled away.

"You are so good," Nikki purred.

"No, you are the one that tastes great." Chance stated. Nikki's shoulder bumped him.

Nikki smiled at the memory of that night with Chance. She noticed it had started raining. In the distance, she could see the lightning.

"Shit, this could be a rough ride," she mumbled.

The rain started to hit the plane harder as it rained harder. The lightning was closer to the plane now. The plane was bouncing a little more from the storm.

The closer Nikki got, the storm grew stronger. She started to hit turbulence. The plane was now bouncing up and down harder and more frequently. The plane almost felt like a yeo-yeo going up and down. Nikki was becoming a little nervous at the intensity of the storm.

Nikki checked the ordinance to see where she was at. She had about another hour before she could land in Mexico. The lightning was now lighting up the ski every few seconds. Nikki radioed the nearest tower and gave them her location. They told Nikki she was flying into a hell of a nasty storm and was advised of her land. She needed to land. The plane was really bouncing around now.

Nikki heard some boxes roll around in the back. The tower gave her the accordance she needed to land. Nikki set the accordance with what they told her. She was feeling anxious about the storm. Nikki started to fly at a lower altitude.

The plane still was bouncing up and down. Nikki hoped the shipment was all right. She knew some of it had broken loose. Nikki landed the plane a little bumpy but on all wheels. She called the tower to find where to park the plane and ride out the storm.

Nikki headed to one of the warehouses. She parked the plane. The storm was still brewing outside. It was down, pouring hard and lightning. The wind had picked up speed. Nikki could hardly see out the plane window.

Nikki had told the tower she would leave as soon as the storm ended. She decided she better check the shipment. Nikki climbed out of the pilot seat and headed to the back of the plane. Nikki noticed one of the boxes laid on its side broke open. There were a couple more tipped over but not broken open. The one that was broke open had white powder pouring out of it. Nikki swallowed hard; she knew it was cocaine. Her heart raced in her chest.

"Fuck!" Nikki yelled and stomped her foot in anger and fear.

"Fuck, fuck," Nikki yelled, knowing now she had been transporting drugs. She wasn't sure what to do. Nikki felt a wave of panic run through her. She would be in a hell of a lot of trouble if customs decided to search her plane. Nikki stared at the Coke, trying to decide what to do with it.

"Fuck, fuck, what do I fucking do? I need to get rid of it." Nikki said. She grabbed the box and turned it upright. The sculpture the cocaine was hidden in had broken open. There were six other sculptures in the box that hadn't broken.

"Shit, shit!" Nikki wondered if they were also stuffed with cocaine. She decided to get rid of the one sculpture and leave the rest alone. Nikki found a plastic bag and put the broken sculpture inside it.

She found a rag and swept up the cocaine off the floor. Nikki put the rag into the plastic bag with the sculpture. The white powder was still on the floor but not as bad as before. Nikki swung the rag around, spreading the rest of the powder around so it looked like dust on the floor.

Nikki looked out the plane window and saw a trash can bedside the warehouse door. She looked around to see if anyone was walking around outside. Nikki didn't see anyone.

Her heart was beating fast from her nerves. The rain was still coming down hard. She had to get rid of the bag. Nikki opened the plane door and climbed out with the bag in her hand. She made sure no one was outside and about. Nikki ran towards the trash can with the bag. She was getting soaked from the rain coming down hard. Nikki opened the lid of the trash can and threw the bag inside. She quickly ran back to the plane.

Nikki climbed back inside the plane. She began to shiver from being soaked by the rain and nerves. Nikki found a towel and wiped the rain from her skin and hair. She sat in the plane's cockpit, chewing her nails in worry. Nikki was feeling anxious and scared. She decided to call Chance.

"Hello, beautiful," Chance said in her ear.

"Hello, sexy man."

"Where are you?" Chance asked, confused, knowing she had a delivery today.

"Sitting in Mexico airport. I am waiting for a terrible storm to blow over."

"Is it bad?"

"Yes, I had to land. The storm was bouncing my plane around like a yeo-yeo."

"Is everything okay?" Chance asked, concerned. Nikki was quiet for a few seconds. "Nikki, what is wrong?"

"Um... I had a box break open in the shipment."

"Okay, but what's got you concerned?"

"Chance, the box....had...um...something in it," Nikki sputtered nervously.

"Nikki, are you implying what I think you are?" Chance asked with concern.

"Um...probably."

"What did you do with it?"

"Cleaned it up and threw it in the trash," Nikki said, biting her fingernail.

Chance felt his heart rate speed up and was sick at her words. Nikki had herself in a hell of a mess. The client would know the box was missing. Nikki watched the trash truck pick up the can, empty it, and then set it back down again.

"Nikki, whoever your shipment was going will know the box is missing."

"I put the box back. All I took out was the broken sculpture. I left the rest in the box."

"Nikki, you have to put it back in the box. Even if it is broken."

"I can't," Nikki squeaked, feeling panic.

"Why?" Chance asked, concerned.

"The trash was just picked up where I put the sculpture in." Nikki swallowed hard. Chance was silent.

"Fuck!" Chance whispered under his breath.

"Chance, I am feeling anxious and panicky. I actually made a mistake, didn't I?"

"You shouldn't have touched the box, Nikki."

"It was all over the floor of the plane. I was afraid someone would come and check out my plane, like customs. Then I would be arrested."

"Shit, this is not good."

"Chance, I am terrified now. I had no idea Hector was using me to fly drugs," Nikki cried, tears rolling down her face.

"Shush, babe. Be careful of what you say."

"Chance, what am I going to do?" Nikki cried. Chance was silent for a few minutes, thinking about the situation.

"Nikki, when are you supposed to arrive in Costa Rica?"

"I am supposed to be there around 5:00–6:00 pm. But I ran into the storm, which put me back a couple of hours."

"Damn, I wish I would have gone with you."

"I wish you would have too."

"Nikki, how long have you been flying for Hector?"

"Um...for about six months. Hector pays me very well."

"I am sure he does; how much?"

"Um...$50-$75 thousand in cash," Nikki whispered. Chance again was silent. That definitely was great money. Chance could understand why Nikki took the job, a single woman with a new plane to pay for.

"Hector likes how reliable and dependable I am. I never ask questions. I just deliver the shipment and never ask for anything more."

"Okay, that could be one advantage. Hector knows you are not going through the shipment. He can trust you to a point."

"This is the first time I have ever had a problem."

"Okay, that could work towards your advantage also."

"I could tell them the sculpture broke, and I threw it away, not knowing anything."

"Nikki, you know them better than I do. Do you think they would believe you?"

"Yes, and I could offer to pay for the damaged sculpture." Nikki noticed the rain was slowing down. She was going to leave soon. If she stayed the night, she would take the chance of having her plane searched.

"Chance, the storm is clearing up. I will have to leave soon or take the chance of having my plane searched."

"Nikki, please wait. I'll fly to where you are and go with you the rest of the way."

"Chance, the tower just said I was in the clear to leave."

"Nikki gave me all the information about where you will be. I'll book a flight and meet you there."

"Chance, this my problem, not yours. I don't want to drag you into this mess."

"Please let me help you, Nik. This could be very dangerous."

"Chance, I was in the Air Force too. I can handle this myself. I'll figure this out."

"Baby, please, I already found a flight. I could be there in four hours."

"No, Chance, this is my problem, not yours. I should have been more careful but I liked the money too much to take precautions. So I have to fix this."

"Nikki, I care a lot about you; please let me help."

"I like you too, but this is still my problem, not yours. I have to go; the tower just cleared me to leave."

"Nikki, call me as soon as you land, promise."

" I will. Thank you, Chance."

"Nikki, please let me help you, " Chance asked again.

"I have to go. I am lined up on the runway. Goodbye, Chance," Nikki said, hanging up her phone. Tears were running down her cheeks. She wished Chance was here with her whole heart. She was scared, but this was her mess, not Chance's. Nikki didn't want to get Chance involved. The piper paid, so she would have to pay the price for the mess up. Nikki sighed heavily, revved the engine, and shot down the runway.

Chapter 9

Nikki arrived in Costa Rica around 10:00pm. She was about four hours late. She parked her plane in the Stamos-owned warehouse. Nikki was feeling very anxious and nervous. She called Juan and Joseph to let them know she was there.

"Hello," Juan said.

"Hey, Juan, it is Nikki. I just arrived at the warehouse with your shipment." Nikki stated.

"We will be there in an hour. Do not leave the warehouse, Nikki." Juan stated firmly.

"I will be right here waiting," Nikki replied.

Juan and Joseph didn't want the shipment to sit in the warehouse overnight. Nikki sat inside her plane, waiting for them to get there. She was trying to decide if she should call Chance again. She decided to text him instead.

Here in Costa Rica, 10:00pm. Everything is fine. See you in a couple of days. Love Nikki.

Nikki sat inside the plane, worried about what Juan and Joseph would say about the broken box. She chewed on her nails, waiting. Nikki heard a car pull up to the warehouse. Her heart started to beat faster with nervousness. She was debating about telling them right away about the broken box or waiting until they checked the shipment.

Nikki could just act like nothing had happened. She cleaned the plane up, so they would only know the box had broken open once they checked the shipment and did inventory.

Nikki started to shake from being so nervous. She needed to come to a decision before they came inside the warehouse. Nikki took a deep breath to calm herself down. She then heard the warehouse door open up. Nikki put a smile on her face. She climbed out of the plane.

"Hello, Joseph," Nikki smiled.

"Nikki, how are you doing?" Joseph smiled, walking towards her.

"I am doing great. How about yourself?"

"Fine. What happened that you are four hours late?"

"I hit a bad storm in Mexico. I had to land for several hours to wait it out." Nikki stated, watching the men unload the cargo from her plane. Joseph stared at Nikki, then nodded his head.

"No other problems?" Joseph asked.

"No, Mexico let me land without checking out the plane since I was going to leave as soon as the weather permitted. I stayed on the plane waiting for the storm to clear, then took off as soon as there was clearance." Nikki stated. Joseph glances over at her curiously, watching her intently. Nikki shifted her stance under his gaze. He was making her more uncomfortable.

"No one checked your plane?" Joseph asked again.

"Why would they. I was just waiting for clearance to leave again. There was no reason for the airport to board my plane. Is something wrong, Joseph?" Nikki asked, smiling. Joseph was silent for a few minutes, then shook his head no.

"No, I was just curious."

"Well, I really need to go to a hotel. I am hungry and tired after the flight here. The storm bounced me around, so I am a little fatigued."

"You are welcome to stay at the main house if you would like."

"Thank you, Joseph, but there are a couple of things I want to do while I am here. I have some friends I am going to see while I am here."

"All right then, I will see you later," Joseph walked towards the door.

Nikki watched him leave and breathed out a sigh of relief. Joseph had her worried for a few minutes with his questions. Nikki called for a taxi to pick her up. Half an hour later, she was at the Grand Costa Rica Hotel. She put her luggage on the bed and began to undress.

Nikki entered the bathroom, reached in, and turned the shower on. She waited a few seconds, then climbed inside the shower, letting the hot water beat over her skin. After a few minutes, Nikki felt her muscles relax a little bit. She washed up, turned the water off, and climbed out, wrapping a towel around her naked body.

Nikki knew she should call Chance, but she was just too tired. Her emotions were too raw after the stress of the day. Nikki dried off, then pulled the covers back on the bed, climbing inside. She texted Chance quickly.

Everything is fine going to bed. Love Nikki.

Nikki put her phone on the stand next to the bed. Nikki curled in a ball wishing Chance was here to hold her tight, waiting for sleep to take over.

Chapter 10

Chance was so upset after talking to Nikki that he called Carter concerned. Chance knew Nikki had gotten herself into a dangerous mess. Nikki had no idea what she got herself into. Chance was really worried about her.

"Chance, what's up?" Carter asked.

"Carter, Nikki has got herself into a serious mess."

"Okay, what kind of mess?"

"She has been flying shipments to Costa Rica for Hector Stamos." Chance stated. Carter was silent for a few seconds.

"Why would Hector Stamos? Never mind. Nikki was transporting drugs and didn't know it, right?"

"Yes, Hector has been paying her excellent money. So she never questioned him. Nikki really didn't know who Hector was to suspect him of anything illegal."

"I am sure Hector was paying good money. What happened to change this?"

"Nikki was delivering a shipment tonight. She ended up in a bad storm in Mexico and had to land. One box broke open and leaked white powder on the floor."

"Shit, Chance, what did she do with it?"

"Nikki realized it was cocaine. She cleaned it up and disposed of the sculpture that held the coke. She put the box back together."

"They will know it is missing and has been tampered with."

"I know; Nikki wouldn't let me go there to meet her. She said it was her problem and would handle it."

"Chance, Nikki could be in a lot of trouble. She is dealing with a big drug cartel."

"I know, but Nik feels she can handle it. Nik has been flying them shipments for six months and never realized what she was dealing with."

"Well, it doesn't matter now. Nikki definitely knows now. She is reliable to them. Nikki really has to be careful how she approaches this problem."

"Carter, I am afraid of what will happen to her. If they don't believe her, Nikki is dead."

"You are right about that. So what are you thinking?"

"I need to go to Costa Rica,"

"You are not going alone and need one of us with you. Chance, you have never dealt with people like this before. Colin would be the best choice since he has been in Guatemala, Nicaragua, and Costa Rica. Colin has dealt with guerrilla warfare and knows people down there." Carter stated firmly. Chance heard his phone buzz with a text.

"Just a minute, Carter. I have a text coming through."

Everything is fine going to bed. Love Nikki.

Chance read the text from Nikki. He still didn't feel relaxed about it.

"I just received a text from Nikki saying everything is fine, but for how long."

"Call Colin, tell him what you are dealing with. Then let me know what your decision is."

"Okay, talk to you in a few." Chance replied, hanging up with Carter. Chance decided to text Nikki back before he called Colin.

Where are you?.... Chance

At the Grand Costa Rica Hotel....Nikki

What happened?.... Chance

Nothing didn't tell.....Nikki

They will know...Chance

Turning a blind eye.....Nikki

Dangerous...Chance

No matter what I do will be dangerous. I am a liability.....Nikki

True, I am coming to get you.....Chance

No don't want you involved...Nikki
Too late and bad...Chance
No, please don't.....Nikki
See you tomorrow...Chance
Please...Nikki
Not option, good night...Chance

Nikki was frustrated with Chance but yet was a little relieved he was coming. She started to relax and fell fast asleep from exhaustion and worry.

Chance called Colin, not getting any answer. He looked at the time. It was 11:30pm. Either Colin was out or in bed sleeping. Chance would have to call him in the morning. Chance decided to go ahead and book a flight for tomorrow at 11:00am.

Chance decided to take a shower to help him relax. He took a quick shower and then climbed into bed. When he finally relaxed enough to fall asleep, Chance dreamed of being in Afghanistan.

Chance was back in the rescue helicopter. Next to him was supposed to be Dean, but he was now Nikki. They had a call to pick up some injured men. The wounded men were located in a heavy war zone. This was the first Dean/Niki ever flew under heavy artillery fire. From the helicopter, they could see the gunfire and the explosives going off all around on the ground below them.

"How will we pick them up with all the firing going on? We will end up getting shot down," Nikki said nervously.

"That is the chance we have to take and train for. There are injured men down there that need help. Without our help, they could die."

"Oh shit! I think we need to turn around." Nikki said nervously.

"No! We have injured men to pick up. They depend on us to pick them up and return them to the hospital." Chance said, lowering the helicopter. The gunfire grew louder the closer they got to the ground. Chance heard Nikki cry out in pain. Chance glanced over at her. She was slumped over in her seat. Nikki's chin was on her chest.

"Nikki, talk to me. Are you all right?" Chance yelled, reaching out to her.

Nikki wasn't moving or talking to him. Chance saw the injured men on the ground, flagging him to land. Chance lowered the helicopter to the ground. Once on the ground, he turned his attention back to Nikki as the men started loading up the injured.

"Nikki, talk to me." Chance yelled, shaking her arm.

Nikki still hadn't moved. Chance grabbed her arm. She slumped over towards him. Chance then noticed the side of her head had a bullet hole. Blood started running down her beautiful face. Her eyes stared out blankly.

"Fuck, no, Nikki!" Chance screamed out."Nikki, no! Please, god, no!"

Chance woke up startled. He had sweat pouring off his body. His body was trembling from the dream. Chance ran his hands through his hair and down his face. His heart was racing, and he was breathing heavily.

"Holy fuck!" Chance whispered to himself.

Chance laid back down, trying to calm himself down. He was really worried about Nikki. He didn't think Nikki realized what a dangerous situation she was really in. They would not just let her walk away. Nikki was a liability to them.

Chapter 11

Chance got up the following day and started packing. He needed to call Colin, then Carter. After he had finished packing, he made some coffee and then called Colin. Colin came over to Chance's house a half hour later.

"Hey, Chance, what's up?" Colin asked.

"I have a huge problem that I need help with."

"Okay, tell me," Colin replied with concern.

"Nikki has been doing deliveries for Hector Stamos for six months."

"Wait, Chance, does Nikki know Hector Stamos is under the suspicion of moving drugs?"

"Nikki knows now. She was doing a delivery to Costa Rica last night. She hit some bad weather in Mexico and had to land. One of the boxes fell over and spilled coke all over the plane's floor."

"Oh fuck, what happened?" Colin didn't like what he heard from Chance.

"Nikki cleaned the mess up. She threw the coke and sculpture it was in the trash. The trash was picked up."

"Holy shit, Chance, she should have left it alone. They are going to know it is missing."

"I know Nikki panicked. She wasn't thinking, now I believe she is going to be in trouble. I would like you to fly to Costa Rica with me. Carter said you would be the best one to go with me." Chance stated. Colin was silent for a few minutes.

"Chance, was Nikki delivering the shipment to Juan and Joseph Stamos?"

"I believe so; why?"

"There might be a problem if I go with you."

"Why?"

"Well, when I was in the Marines, we were trying to infiltrate into the human slavery ring. We believe Juan Stamos is one of the main men involved in Costa Rica. I posed as a buyer in disguise."

"Holy shit, Colin, I didn't know that." Chance was surprised at Colin's comment.

"We were trying to find a congressman's daughter. She was 20 years old at the time when she was abducted. Juan and his crew moved the girls fast. We couldn't nail him or find the congressman's daughter."

"Wait a minute, Colin. This might work to our advantage. You know as well as I do; they aren't going to let Nikki walk away."

"Yes, you are probably right. Nikki is now a liability to them."

"Colin, what do you think they will do to her?" Chance asked, concerned. Colin stared at him in silence, thinking.

"They will either kill her or put her into the sex slavery ring," Colin stated softly. Chance felt his stomach tighten into a knot at Colin's words. They both were silent for a few minutes.

"Colin, would you consider posing as a buyer again. Nikki could be your stepsister or something like that." Chance suggested. It could work. Colin stood still, thinking about what Chance had just mentioned.

"Chance, that could work. They might not hurt Nikki, then. I will call a couple of contacts and let them know I am going to Costa Rica. That way, my identity will be all set there."

"Will you be ready by 11:00am? to fly out with me?"

"That will not give me enough time to get ready. Can you rebook the flight to the last flight out?"

"I can do one better. I will call Dean and get us a plane. Then we can leave when everything is all set with you."

"Great, I will call you when I am ready." Colin headed towards the door.

After Colin left, Chance called Carter to tell him what was happening. A half-hour later, Chance called Nikki. Her cell phone went to voice mail. He redialed her number, and the same thing happened. He felt his stomach tighten again and felt nauseous with worry.

Chapter 12

Nikki woke up to the sound of someone pounding on her hotel door. Nikki climbed out of bed and got dressed. She walked to the door and looked through the peephole. Juan Stamos was at her door. Nikki felt a wave of nervousness. Nikki swallowed hard, taking a deep breath before opening up the door. She put on a smile and opened the door facing Juan Stamos.

Juan Stamos was a handsome man with dark Italian looks. He had short black hair with dark eyes. He wore a goatee and a mustache on his handsome face. Juan stood about 5"11 with a lean muscular body. He was dressed in a silver suit that fit his frame to perfection. Juan always looked like he should be on the cover of CQ magazine.

"Juan, what on earth are you doing here?" Nikki asked, smiling.

"I came to bring you to the house for breakfast."

"Oh, that isn't necessary. I have plans for meeting friends today."

"Oh, I must insist. We have another business proposal we would like to discuss with you."

"Um...okay. I guess that would be all right. Just let me change real quickly."

"Nikki, you look beautiful as always."

"Thank you, but I do need to freshen up first."

"Fine, but don't take too long," Juan stated firmly, walking into her hotel room uninvited.

Nikki smiled and walked into the bathroom. Her hands were shaking from her nerves. She grabbed some nicer clothes and put them on. She then went into the bathroom and turned on the water. She started to text Chance.

It is 9:00am. Juan showed up at the hotel. Want to talk business over breakfast at his house. Not sure if he knows about the missing sculpture. Call me when you land. Nikki.

Nikki shut off the water and went back into the bedroom. She slipped her cell phone into her purse. Nikki wrote down Juan's address and put it in her suitcase. She grabbed her purse and walked out to the living room. Juan was sitting on the sofa, waiting for her patiently. He smiled and stood up when she came out of the bedroom.

"Ready?" Juan asked.

"Yes," Nikki nodded her head. She had an awful feeling about going with Juan. She had a strong urge to turn around, run back into the room, and lock the door. Nikki swallowed hard and walked to the elevator with Juan from the hotel room.

Juan had his hand at the small of her back, guiding her to the elevator. There was a limo waiting for them in front of the hotel. Juan glided Nikki to the limo. The driver opened the back door for them. Nikki climbed inside first, then Juan followed her inside.

"Juan, I have to be back at the hotel by noon. I have a friend flying here to spend a few days with me, then we are meeting another couple for dinner tonight."

"Not to worry. I will have you back in time. Who is the friend flying in?"

"His name is Chance. We have been seeing each other for a couple of months."

"That is nice. Does this person know you work for my father?"

"He knows I have a flying business but doesn't know who my clients are."

"What does he do for a living?"

"He installs security systems."

"Does he do houses and businesses?"

"Yes, both."

"Great."

The limo turned into the Stamos' driveway that headed to a huge mansion. Nikki swallowed hard from her nerves. She hid her hands from Juan so he wouldn't see them shaking in her lap. The limo pulled up in front of the house.

The limo driver climbed out and opened the back door for them. Juan climbed out first and held his hand out to Nikki. Nikki grabbed his hand and climbed out of the limo. Juan led her to the front door. They walked into the house.

Joseph and two other men were sitting in the living room. Joseph stood up when they walked into the room. Joseph looked a lot like Juan, except Joseph had long hair pulled back into a ponytail. Joseph also sported a goatee and mustache. Joseph smiled at Nikki.

"Nikki, how nice you could join us for breakfast. I believe Maria has it already. Let's go sit in the dining room," Joseph smiled, then leaned in, kissing Nikki's cheek.

"Thank you, Joseph," Nikki smiled.

They all walked out to the dining table and sat down. Maria served the food. They all eat quietly. Nikki wasn't hungry at all from being so nervous, pushing the food around her plate. She noticed Juan and Joseph exchanging glances. They all finished eating; Juan sat back in his chair and crossed his long legs, staring at Nikki. Nikki glanced up from her plate and smiled at him.

"What happened last night, Nikki?" Juan asked, smiling.

"I had to land in Mexico because of the bad storm. That was why I was a few hours late." Nikki replied. Juan glanced at Joseph.

"Did anything happen to the shipment?" Joseph asked.

"What do you mean?" Nikki asked nervously, feeling her heart race, twisting her napkin in her lap underneath the table.

"So nothing happened to the shipment. It was the same as you received it?" Juan asked.

"As far as I know, I landed in Mexico and waited for the storm to clear. As soon as it was clear, I headed here." Nikki stated. Juan and Joseph looked at each other again.

"Juan, is something wrong?" Nikki asked.

"Yes, a sculpture is missing from the shipment," Juan stated.

Nikki swallowed hard, twisting her hand tighter around the napkin. She now knew they had found the shipment had been tampered with. Nikki twisted the napkin around her fingers so tightly that they were beginning to hurt. She loosened them a little.

"Are you sure it was in the shipment? Maybe someone forgot to pack it." Nikki said softly. Again the brothers exchanged a look. Joseph cleared his throat.

"Nikki, you have been doing deliveries for us for six months. We have never had a problem until now. The sculpture was packed in the shipment. We have confirmation everything was packed very carefully and doubled checked," Joseph stated firmly.

Nikki nervously twisted the napkin tighter in her lap again. She was deciding whether to tell them the truth or not.

"Nikki, we think a lot of you, but we will not tolerate someone stealing from us," Juan stated firmly. Nikki's head snapped up quickly, and they looked over at Juan.

"I would never steal anything from you. During the storm, the plane was bouncing all over. One of the boxes crashed over and broke open. When I landed in Mexico, I noticed the mess. The sculpture shattered. I cleaned up the mess it made and threw it away in the nearby trash bend." Nikki said. Juan looked at Joseph and laughed.

"Joseph, can you believe Nikki threw a sculpture away worth $200,000.00," Juan replied, laughing. Joseph shook his head in disbelief.

"Oh my god! I had no idea it was worth that much. It was a vase. Did you have insurance on it?" Nikki said in shock.

"Yes, the vase was worth that much. Now we are out $200,000.00," Juan stated firmly.

"Can't you turn it into your insurance? I can sign the report that it was damaged on the plane due to a storm." Nikki said. Juan started laughing, and Joseph joined in. Nikki watched them feeling sick to her stomach. She swallowed hard, feeling her heart race.

"What is so funny? You do carry insurance on something that is that valuable, right?" Nikki asked.

"Well, yes, generally, but this shipment wasn't insured," Joseph replied.

"Why not if it was so valuable?" Nikki asked.

Juan suddenly stood up. He was angry and walked over to Nikki. He grabbed her face firmly in his hand. Juan's finger's dug into her skin, hurting her. Nikki could see the anger on his face. His eyes were slanted and cold, and his lips were in a thin tight line, sneering.

"I am done playing games with you, Nikki. Where is the fucking vase?" Juan sneered in her face.

"I...told you...it broke on the plane. I threw it in the trash at the airport," Nikki sputtered out as fear raced through her.

Juan let go of her face and then backhanded her hard across the face. Nikki's head turned to the side from the blow. Searing pain raced across her face. Her hands instantly went to her face. Tears come to her eyes as the string spreads on her skin. Nikki was surprised Juan had just backhanded her.

"You fucking bitch! You threw $200,000.00 worth of cocaine in the fucking trash," Juan yelled and backhanded her again. Nikki cried out in pain.

"The sculpture broke and made a mess. There was dust from the sculpture breaking on the floor, so I cleaned it up." Nikki cried out.

"Did you not just fucking hear me, Nikki. It was $200,000.00 worth of fucking cocaine," Juan yelled.

"Didn't know; I thought it was dust from the sculpture." Nikki cried.

Juan grabbed her by the hair and pulled her head back so she was looking straight up at him as he towered over her. Her body trembled with fear. Nikki didn't know what was coming next. Chance had forewarned she was in a dangerous situation.

"You want me to fucking believe that you didn't know the vase held cocaine. For the last six months, you have been doing deliveries to us, and never once have you ever questioned what you were delivering," Juan yelled in her face. Nikki swallowed hard before replying. Tears rolled down her cheeks as she shook her head.

"No, Hector paid me well. I didn't have a reason to be suspicious of anything. I am telling you the truth," Nikki cried out. Juan started pacing the length of the table in anger.

"Why should we believe you, Nikki?" Joseph asked calmly, staring at her with his arms folded across his chest. Nikki turned to look at him. She swallowed hard and brushed the tears from her face.

"Your father paid me $50 to $75 thousand in cash to make the deliveries. I have never recorded the money. So there is no trace of the deliveries, money, or your father. I have never ever asked Hector what was in the shipments. I didn't know what to lose the money or him as a client."

"You never suspected you were delivery drugs?" Joseph asked. Nikki shook her head no. "Then what do you think you were delivering?"

"Hector told me the shipment involved expensive art and material. When he first approached me, Hector showed me the art and material that would be delivered. I had no reason to think it was anything different."

"You never, out of curiosity, looked in the boxes?" Joseph asked.

"No, I never had a reason to. Your father paid me well," Nikki stated. Joseph nodded his head to her. Juan still was pacing around angrily.

"Joseph, we are still out $200,000.00," Juan said sharply.

Joseph looked at Juan nodding his head in agreement. Nikki sat watching them feeling nauseous. She had to keep swallowing or vomiting. Her body was shaking from nerves and fear. Her face stung and burned where Juan had backhanded her. Nikki was afraid of what they were going to do to her. Juan suddenly stopped pacing and turned quickly to face Nikki.

"You will stay here for a couple of days until Joseph and I figure out what to do about this problem," Juan stated. Nikki was startled by his statement.

"Roger, take Nikki upstairs," Juan stated firmly.

"Juan, I can't stay here. I am supposed to meet with friends today," Nikki sputtered out. Juan turned towards her, glaring.

"You expect us to just let you leave when you now owe us $200,000.00," Juan asked furiously. "Take her upstairs, now!"

The guy named Roger grabbed Nikki by the arm, forcefully pulling her up out of the chair.

"Please, Juan. I really need to get back to the hotel. My boyfriend is flying in today. I promise I will not leave until I hear from you." Nikki pleaded, not liking where this situation was going. Juan nodded his head to Roger.

"Get her out my fucking sight," Juan yelled out.

"Please, Juan, don't do this. I am sorry. I will find a way to pay the money back for your stuff," Nikki cried out, trying to pull her arm from Roger's tight grip. Juan just waved his hand in the air.

Roger firmly gripped her arm, pulling her to the stairs. Nikki tried to pull out of his grip, but he held her tighter.

"No, please!" Nikki cried out.

Roger pulled her up the stairs. Nikki started to feel really scared. Roger pulled her down the hallway past a dozen of doors. Roger stopped and opened a door. He led Nikki into the room. Roger pushed her further into the room and then turned around, walking quickly to the door. Roger closed the door and locked the door. He stood still and put his finger to his lips.

"Nikki, I am a friend of Colin Black's; his brother is Chance Black," Roger whispered.

"Oh my god! What is going to happen to me?" Nikki replied. Roger put his finger to his lips to shush her.

"Please whisper and try to stay calm. I will let Colin know everything about what is going to take place. Juan is not going to let you walk away from this."

"Oh god, please get me out of here," Nikki said. Roger shook his head.

"Nikki, please listen to me carefully. I can't help you. If I do, I will blow my cover and end up dead. We have been trying to nail Juan and Joseph for three years for drugs and sex trafficking."

"Oh my god!" Nikki sat down on the bed at his statement. She put her head in her hands as tears started to roll down her face. "What is going to happen to me?"

"First, Juan will get you hooked on cocaine. Then you will be put in a sex ring and sold."

"Oh my god! Please get me out of here!" Nikki pleaded with tears rolling down her cheeks.

"I am sorry, Nikki. You will have to trust me. I will keep Colin Black informed of your whereabouts. But I can't break my cover for you." Roger stated firmly. "I have to leave now. Just keep your head and don't do anything stupid. I will do what I can to help you." Roger said, turning around and walking towards the door. He opened the door and walked out, locking the door behind himself.

Nikki heard the door lock from the outside. She sat on the bed with tears rolling down her face. Nikki couldn't believe the mess she got herself into. She had been stupid for not being suspicious, but she really liked the money Hector was paying her.

She knew there was talk of Hector being involved in drugs, but she turned a blind eye. It would take a couple of years to make the kind of money Hector was paying. The money was paying off her plane. With it, she made the steep payments. Now because of the blind eye, she was in trouble with possibly no way out.

Nikki wondered if she was ever going to see Chance again. Her heart ached more with the thought of never seeing or being with Chance. He had given her subtle hints about the shipments when she told him who she was doing deliveries for. But, of course, Nikki wouldn't listen. She knew in her conscience what was in the shipments but buried it. Now she was going to pay for not listening to her conscience. Nikki lay on the bed and let the floodgates open. She cried herself into exhaustion.

Chapter 13

Colin had made a few calls to get information on the Stamos family. He discovered Jackson Adams, aka Roger Belford, was deeply undercover inside the Stamos family. Jackson and Colin had served together. They also had been uncovering together trying to stop sex trafficking. Colin had gotten out, but Jackson had stayed, getting himself in deeper with the Stamos family. Colin's cell phone rang. He didn't recognize the number.

"Hello?" Colin said.

"Hey, Colin, this is Jackson Adams," Jackson said.

"Jackson, what is going on?" Colin asked.

"I told you I would call you about Nikki Curtis, the woman you know."

"Yes, what is going on with Nikki, Jackson?"

"The Stamos brothers know about the situation about the missing product. Your friend is in some serious shitting trouble."

"I figured that. What are they going to do to her?"

"They are discussing putting her into the auction to get back the money they are out."

"Fuck! How much time do I have?"

"Maybe 24 hours or less. They are really pissed off. Juan wanted to kill her, but Joseph talked Juan into selling her at the auction to recoup the money for the product lost."

"Being in the auction is better than death but not much more."

"True."

"I will be there in about six hours. Please keep me informed when you can."

"I will let you know when the auction is."

"Thanks, Jackson." Colin hung up his phone. Chance came into the room, looking at Colin's grim face.

"Colin, are we all set to leave yet?"

"Chance, we need to talk first. I just got a call from Jackson Adams, aka Roger Belford. He is an undercover agent and works for the Stamos brothers. They have Nikki and know about the missing sculpture. The brothers are not going to let her leave their sight. I am sure the product she threw away had a heavy price tag, and they want to recoup it."

"Fuck!" Chance yelled, running his fingers through his short hair. Chance started pacing the kitchen in worry. "Fuck! Colin, now what do we do?"

"Calm down; Jackson will keep me informed on Nikki. I will go down to Costa Rica as Alex Malcolm, sex slave buyer, and you are my brother Daniel Malcolm."

"Okay, then what happens?"

"Chance, you need to understand what is going to happen. Nikki is a liability to them. They will not just let her leave. Nikki is still a young and beautiful woman. They will get her hooked on drugs. That way, they will be able to control her. Nikki will rely on them for the drugs, and then they will sell her in their sex slave auction."

"Fuck Colin!" Chance yelled in frustration.

"Chance, I am telling you all this to get you prepared. I need you to be able to hold it together. The Stamos brothers move girls really fast, so it is hard to find them. There is a chance we might be able to get her back." Colin stated firmly, gripping Chance's shoulder in a firm hold.

"I will hold it together, and we will get her back, Colin."

"You must follow my orders without questions, even if that means leaving Nikki behind. You need to understand what is at stake. Many people are undercover, and we can't blow their covers for Nikki and jeopardize their lives."

"What do you mean, Colin?" Chance asked, startled by his comment.

"It means you can't or will not blow our cover for any reason. There are too many lives that would be affected. Do you understand what I am saying, Chance? Nikki may or may not be coming back with us."

"Yes, I understand what you are saying. I just don't like it." Chance nodded his head.

"I am all packed and ready to go. We have an appointment to get tattoos stenciled on us and a makeover. We won't recognize each other when my guy is done with us."

"Okay," Chance replied.

Chance and Colin were on their way to the airport three hours later. Chance couldn't believe their transformation. Colin's buddy Reggie was a miracle worker. Chance did not even hardly recognize himself, let alone Colin.

They both were sporting tattoos, sleeves on their arms, and piercing in their ears. Colin had to piercing on his eyebrow and nose. They both were sporting long black hair pulled back into a ponytail. They had dark brown eyes instead of blue eyes and a goatee with mustaches. Even their skin was a darker color with a spray tan.

"Colin, I don't think Nikki would even recognize me with this get-up. Hell, I don't even recognize you, let alone myself." Chance stated, looking at Colin with amazement.

"That is the whole point. I have your new identity right here, Daniel Malcolm."

"Thank you, Alex," Chance laughed.

They walked out to the truck, climbed inside, and headed to the airport. Chance had rented a plane for them to fly to Costa Rica. Chance and Colin flew into Cost Rica around 12:00am, in the morning. They checked into the Grand Costa Rica Hotel. The same one Nikki was supposed to be in. Chance had texted her numerous time and had yet to receive a reply.

Chapter 14

Nikki sat on the bed, worried about what Juan and Joseph would do to her next. She didn't like what Roger had told her. Nikki wondered if Chance was in Costa Rica yet. She looked at her watch. It was late in the afternoon.

Nikki heard someone at the bedroom door, hearing the lock turn. She hoped Roger was coming back to get her out of the house and away from the Stamos brothers. The door opened, and Nikki stood up from the bed. Juan and Roger walked inside the room.

Nikki stared at them, seeing the grim look on Roger's face. She saw Roger's mouthed, sorry behind Juan's back. Nikki swallowed hard and weighed her odds if she could make it to the door by passing Juan and escaping. Roger had forewarned what was going to happen. Nikki felt nervous and afraid. Juan stood in front of her, staring at her intently. Roger moved to the side of her.

"What is going on?" Nikki asked nervously.

Juan nodded his head to Roger. Roger moved quickly, gripping Nikki's arm tightly and bending it behind her back. Nikki saw Juan pull a vial and needle out of his pocket. Before Nikki could move or say anything, Juan plunged the needle into her arm. Nikki was startled that Juan just shot her in the arm with something. She looked at Juan with confusion.

"What did you just do to me, Juan?" Nikki asked, worried.

"Just gave you something to make you feel excellent," Juan laughed. Roger let go of her arm.

"What do you mean?" Nikki asked, rubbing her arm with worry.

"I gave you a sample of the coke you decided to dispose of."

"Oh my god! I have never used drugs before. What the hell!" Nikki said, rubbing her arm harder.

"I don't fucking care. You are going to love this and are going to have a great trip?" Juan laughed.

"I don't understand, Juan. I never once stole anything from your family. Call your father. Tell him what happened. I bet Hector would tell you to let me go."

"You really think my father would help you?" Juan laughed harder.

"Yes. I have been loyal. I never once inspected the shipments. I only cleaned up the mess and disposed of the sculpture because I was afraid customs might come onto my plane and inspect it. I didn't know that the mess on the floor was cocaine, not even notice. I thought it was dust from the sculpture breaking."

"You really want me to believe that shit, Nikki?"

"Yes, because it is the truth."

"Then why the fuck did you lie at first?"

"Because I wasn't sure what to do. I figured the sculpture was valuable."

"You still fucking lied, Nikki. What would have happened if the man was killed that packed that box because of stealing product?"

"I didn't think of that because I never thought you and your family were drug lords. I thought your family was just an influential family with a lot of money, nothing else." Nikki started to feel light-headed, feeling her blood rushing through her veins.

"I see you are feeling the effects of the cocaine now. Your eyes are glassy, and you are swaying back and forth. Have a happy trip, Nikki." Juan laughed, walking towards the door.

"Wait....please...Juan." Nikki slurred her words. Juan waved his hand at her, opening up the bedroom door. Juan and Roger walked out of the room. Juan laughed as the door closed behind him.

Nikki slowly walked over to the bed, trying to focus her eyes. Everything seemed to be moving, and she felt unsteady. She felt like she was floating in the air. There were bright, beautiful colors dancing all around her. She kept reaching out, trying to catch the colors in her hand. She had the urge to dance with the colors.

Nikki started to shuffle her feet in a circle while she reached out to touch the colors floating in the air. Nikki forgot about her fear and Juan. Nikki started laughing as she danced around the room with the beautiful colors. Nikki is terrific and worry-free right at the moment. Light as a feather, dancing around the room, laughing.

Chapter 15

After a few days in Costa Rica, Chance retrieved a key to Nikki's hotel room. There had been no sight of Nikki anywhere. They had asked around about anyone seeing an American woman describing Nikki. Of course, no one had seen a woman fitting Nikki's description. Chance had called Carter.

"Hey brother, what's up?" Carter asked.

"We need access to Nikki's room. Hopefully, she left something in her room about where she is." Chance replied

"Still no sign of Nikki?"

"Absolutely nothing. It is like Nikki disappeared in thin air."

"So, what do you need me to do?" Carter asked.

"Can you have Lillie call the Grand Costa Rica Hotel? She needs to pretend like Nikki and get me access to Nikki's room."

"Okay, we can make that happen. Anything else?" Carter asked.

"No, just keep digging for anything on the Stamos family."

"Yep, already doing that. How are you holding up, Chance?"

"I am worried we will not get to Nikki in time, and she will be sent overseas or killed."

"You need to stay positive. Colin is good at what he does."

"I am finding that out. I don't even know my own brother right now. He has a totally different personality and disguise."

"I know it is freaky. Colin sent me pictures of you and him. I didn't even recognize the both of you."

"I am trying hard to trust his judgment, but it is hard."

"Chance, I know it is hard, but remember all the lives at stake if his or your cover is blown."

"I know. I kept reminding myself that we are in a dangerous situation here."

"Colin has worked in this situation before, so listen to him."

"I know, but taking orders from my younger brother is hard."

"I understand, but please listen to him, Chance."

"I will. Thank you, and tell Lillie, thank you."

"Of course. Be careful, please. Lillie just called the hotel for you. She put your name Daniel Malcolm on the room, so now you should be able to get a key."

"Great, thanks, Carter." Chance said, hanging up his cell phone. Colin came walking into the hotel room with breakfast for them. He was carrying a bag with bagels and coffee. Colin sat the bag down on the table and looked at Chance.

"I just got done talking to Carter. Lillie added me to Nikki's room, so I should be able to get a key to her room now."

"Great, you need to eat something before we go to Nikki's room," Colin stated firmly.

"I am not hungry." Chance sat, grabbing the coffee cup.

"You need to eat. You have hardly eaten anything in the last couple of days. You need to keep your strength up for what is coming next."

"What does that mean, Colin?"

"Eat, and I will tell you."

"Fucker, I am not hungry."

"Don't care, fucking eat whether you want to or not. Rule one always keeps your strength. Two, follow your instincts, and three, always be aware of your surroundings and those around you." Colin stated, handing Chance a bagel. "The are different kinds of spread for the bagel if you want some." Colin pointed to several different containers.

Chance grabbed a knife and spread blueberry cream cheese on his bagel. He began to eat before he knew it; he was finished with it. Chance grabbed a second one and ate it. Colin smiled, knowing

Chance had to be hungry since he hadn't eaten much since they landed in Costa Rica.

"Okay, tell me what you found out." Chance said, grabbing a third bagel.

"I have had contact with Roger, aka Jackson Adams. Nikki is at the Stamos house."

"Fine, let's go fucking get her."

"We, of course, cannot. Nikki is being punished for tossing away $200,000.00 worth of cocaine."

"Fuck! Now what?"

"Jackson said for the last couple of days, Juan has been drugging her. She is locked in a bedroom until they decide what to do with her next."

"Son of a bitch, Colin! This fucking sucks. I want to go get Nikki out of there."

"You cannot. The Stamos family would either kill you or make a mule out of you."

"They would have to kill me before I would be a drug runner. The fucking pieces of shit!"

If Nikki left anything in her hotel room, they had already found it. I believe the Stamos brothers would have had her room searched, especially since $200,000.00 worth of cocaine was missing from the shipment. Roger said Juan and Joseph didn't believe her story of the box breaking open and the sculpture broken. Especially Nikki, not knowing it was cocaine on the floor and throwing the mess out."

"Nikki told them the truth after all."

"Evidently not at first; she lied to them and acted like she didn't know about the sculpture missing. She all confessed after they confronted her."

"Shit, it might have gone better if she told them the truth first."

"Maybe. The Stamos brothers might have believed she was naive if she had been honest first. Who knows."

"So, what happens now, Colin?"

"We must wait to see if the Stamos brothers put her in the sex traffic auction."

"Why?"

"Because that will be easier for us to get to Nikki. We cannot get anywhere near Nikki right now at the brother's house. The place is guarded like Fort Knox, and no way to get inside without being caught."

"Jeezus! I don't know if I can do this without losing my shit, Colin."

"I can do this without you, Chance if need be," Colin stated firmly. Chance shook his head.

"No, I can't let Nikki down."

"Then you will need to keep your shit together. It is only getting more dangerous from here on out." Colin stared at Chance. Chance nodded his head in understanding.

"Let's go have a look in Nikki's room. They might have missed something." Colin said. Chance stood up, nodding his head in agreement. They walked to the hotel lobby, so Chance could get the extra key to Nikki's room.

Once Chance had the extra key, he and Colin walked to Nikki's room. Chance unlocked the door, and they walked inside the room. Nikki's personal perfume scent hit Chance as he walked into the room. His stomach clenched in a knot with the scent wrapping around him.

"Fuck!" Chance said softly. Colin looked at Chance with curiosity. "I can smell her perfume."

"Ah... yes, you are right," Colin said, sniffing the air.

Chance walked into the bedroom seeing Nikki's suitcase on the bed. He walked over to it and opened it. Chance brushed his hand over her clothes. Everything looked up untouched. Chance sighed, not liking the idea of going through her personal stuff. Chance took a deep breath and started to move her clothes around. He found a small piece of paper in the back pocket of her jeans. It had an address on it. Chance wondered if it was the Stamos brother's address. He put the piece of paper in his pocket. Chance checked the rest of her stuff and found nothing else.

"Did you find anything?" Colin asked in the doorway.

"Just an address, but there was no name on it." Chance replied.

"I didn't find anything," Colin stated.

"That was all found." Chance said.

"Okay, let's head out then," Colin stated. Chance nodded his head. They walked out of the hotel room.

Chapter 16

Nikki woke up every day for a week feeling like shit, wearing the same gray sweatsuit. She had a cottonmouth with a horrible headache. Nikki went into the bathroom to rinse her mouth out. She knew it was from the drugs Juan had been shooting in her arm. Nikki fucking hated it when he would come into the room with a fucking smug smile. She tried to escape from him and Roger every time, but it was useless. Now her body craved the fucking shit. Her hands were shaking, and her skin felt like it was crawling. Nikki wasn't even sure what day it was or if it was still the first day when she arrived.

Nikki sat on the bed, rubbing her arms and legs. She stood up and began pacing the room. Nikki started to have anxiety and couldn't stay still. She knew what her body was craving already. She needed Juan to come with the drugs. Nikki didn't even know how many times Juan had given her the cocaine. All she knew was she craved it badly now.

Nikki paced the room, hoping Juan would come soon before she went crazy with want. It was all she could think about right now. Nikki couldn't keep her mind focused on anything else. She tried, but her mind would go back to wondering where Juan was and if he would bring her a fix. Her mouth watered at the thought of her next fix.

Nikki never understood how people could do drugs, but now she did. The cocaine made her feel great. She loved the feel of it rushing through her body. It made her body feel alive and more sensitive. She would lose track of time. Time didn't matter except when the buzz began to wear off, and you needed another fix.

Nikki heard the lock on the door disengage. Nikki rushed to the door with excitement. She almost felt like jumping up and down like a child. Juan came through the door. He had a package under his arm. Juan smiled at Nikki.

"I have something for you," Juan smiled and handed her the box. Nikki smiled and took the box, hoping it was what her body craved. She sat down on the bed.

“Open it, Nikki,” Juan said. Nikki nodded her head.

She opened the box. Nikki needed clarification on what was in the box. It wasn't what she wanted. She pulled out a sheer white nightgown. There was also a pair of white high-heeled sandals in the box. Nikki looked at Juan with puzzlement. It wasn't the coke she craved.

“Do you like it, Nikki?” Juan asked.

“Um...it is beautiful...but what is it for?” Nikki asked with confusion.

“For you, love. You will be wearing it tonight.”

“Um...I don’t know.” Nikki felt so confused. She knew Juan was married. So why did he give her this sexy gown?

"Well, love, it is time to pay me back for the coke you disposed of," Juan said, smiling. Nikki looked at Juan with a startled look. She put the gown back into the back.

"Um...I don't..." Nikki started to say when Juan grabbed her by the arms. She was facing him and could see the anger on his face.

"Oh, you will, love, make no mistake about it. You have no choice. You owe me $200,000.00, and I intend to collect it. You will soak in a nice bath and get nice and clean. My personal assistant will come in to help you get ready. After you are ready, I will come back for you." Juan stated.

Nikki was feeling very uncomfortable with the idea. Juan pressed a vial into her hand. Her heartbeat was faster at the feel of the vial in her hand.

"This will tie you over until I come back for you. Then I will bring you more, love." Juan whispered in her ear. "I want you all smooth and silky. So make sure you shave your whole body."

Juan kissed her on the lips. He quickly turned to leave and walked out the door. As soon as the door closed and locked, Nikki rushed to the dresser. She felt the excitement of having the coke. She almost dropped the vial with her shaking hands.

Nikki made four lines and then cut the coke like Juan had taught her. She sighed in relief, looking at the lines of coke on the dresser. Nikki bent down and snorted the coke into her nose. She moaned at the feel of coke burning her nose and rushing through her body. She snorted all four lines.

After Nikki snorted the coke, she heard the door open. A small Mexican woman came into the room with a smile. She nodded to Nikki and then headed to the bathroom. Nikki listened to the water turn in the bathroom. She lay on the bed staring at the ceiling, watching the colors dancing. She heard the woman come out of the bathroom.

"Miss, your bath is ready." The woman said.

"I don't want to take a bath right now. I am watching the pretty colors dance on the ceiling," Nikki said, pointing at the ceiling. The woman looked up at the ceiling.

"I don't see any colors, Miss." The woman stated.

"I do, and they are beautiful," Nikki said, smiling.

"Please, Miss, Mr. Stamos gave strict orders for me to get you ready."

"I don't care. Mr. Stamos is a married man."

"Please, Miss, come into the bathroom for your bath."

"Fine, what is your name?" Nikki asked, looking at the woman.

"Anna, please follow me, Miss."

"Anna, I feel like dancing."

"Please, dance your way to the bathroom."

"Fine, fine, Anna." Nikki danced around the room, twirling in circles. Anna stood still and watched her dance. Nikki laughed. "Come join me, Anna."

"Miss, you really need to get into the bathtub before someone comes and checks on us."

"You are a Debbie downer."

"No, my name is Anna, not Debbie."

"I know that silly girl. That was just a phrase."

"Okay, come, Miss."

Anna pointed to the bathroom as Nikki danced towards it. Nikki finally went inside the bathroom. She walked over to the sunken bathtub reaching down to feel the water. The water was warm with lots of bubbles.

"Look at all the fluffy white bubbles," Nikki said, grabbing a handful and bringing them to her mouth. She blew the bubbles off her hand towards Anna. Nikki laughed as the bubble cluster landed on Anna's head. Anna smiled.

"Please, Miss, get undressed and into the tub," Anna stated.

"Fine, Miss bossy pants," Nikki said. Nikki pulled off the sweatshirt and sweatpants Roger had given her. She had not bothered to change her clothes, bathe, brush her hair, or even look in a mirror. Waiting and getting the cocaine from Juan was more important.

Nikki stepped into the water and then sank down. The water came up her breasts. Nikki smiled, grabbing handfuls of bubbles like a child and blowing the clusters all over, laughing.

"Miss, we need to shave the hair from your body," Anna stated. Nikki looked at her laughing.

"Are you going to shave my body, Anna?" Nikki asked.

"Of course, Miss," Anna replied.

"Have at it then," Nikki said, raising her leg and resting it on the tub's edge. Anna grabbed the razor, put lotion on Nikki's leg, and shaved her legs.

An hour later, Nikki was clean-shaven and refreshed. After another couple of hours of fussing, Nikki was finally finished being pampered. She stood in front of the mirror. Nikki was amazed at what Anna had done to her. Her makeup and hair were done to perfection.

Nikki felt beautiful; she wished it was all for Chance, not Juan. The sheer nightgown showed off her body. The gown shimmered in the light when she turned. Juan didn't give her any panties to go under the gown.

“Anna, where are the panties?” Nikki asked. Anna shook her head.

"I am not sure, Miss," Anna replied.

"I need some panties on," Nikki stated. Anna strolled over to the dresser, pulling it open. Anna shook her head no.

"I am sorry, Miss, but there are none here," Anna replied.

"Okay," Nikki said, sitting on the edge of the bed, twisting her hands together. Her mind went to Chance, wishing he would be the one to see her in this beautiful nightgown without any panties. She missed him and wondered if she would ever see and touch him again. Nikki tried to remember the last time she saw or heard Chance's sexy deep voice. She thought it had only been a few days but didn't realize it had been over a week.

Nikki remembered her phone was in her purse. She stood up and began looking around the room for her purse. Nikki started to feel frantic when she couldn't find it. She knew she had brought it with her into the room. It was now missing.

“Miss, what are you looking for?” Anna asked.

"My purse. It was here when Juan brought me to this room. I need to make a phone call."

"Um...Miss, there is nothing in this room that belongs to you." Anna stated.

"Fuck, Juan must have taken it," Nikki said as her mind switched channels. She forgot about Chance and her purse, wondering if Juan would bring her more cocaine. Nikki could use another fix, especially if she was going to have sex with Juan. She would just have to imagine it was Chance instead of Juan.

Nikki heard someone at the bedroom door. She felt a wave of anxiety and happiness. The door opened; Juan walked into the room with Roger trailing behind him. Juan had on a nice tailored black suit. He looked like a model on the cover of a magazine.

Juan smiled at Nikki as his eyes traveled over her from head to foot. He made a twirl sign with his finger for her to turn around for him. Nikki slowly turned around for him in a circle.

"You are very lovely and breathtakingly gorgeous, Nikki," Juan said, nodding his head in approval. "Anna, you have done a fantastic job."

"Thank you, Mr. Stamos," Anna said, smiling. Roger held out a wade of money for Anna. Anna took the money and then walked out of the room.

Juan walked towards Nikki and held out his hands to her. Nikki placed her hand in his. Juan quickly grabbed her arm and plunged a needle into her. Nikki was startled.

"What are you giving me, Juan," Nikki said with concern.

"You, love, will bring in some serious money tonight," Juan stated.

"What do you mean?" Nikki asked, feeling nervous.

"At the auction tonight, that is how you will pay me back. You, love, are going to be sold to the highest bidder."

Nikki finally understood and felt a wave of panic wash over her. She jerked her arm away from Juan. This was why she was dressed in a nightgown and high-heeled shoes. Nikki tried to move away from Juan, but she was feeling really lightheaded. Her eyes began to become unfocused. Everything around her became distorted looking.

"What is happening to me?" Nikki mumbled as she started to fall. Juan had caught her before Nikki fell to the ground. Nikki collapsed against him, mumbling.

“Feel....so.... strange.” She slurred.

"You are going to sell for a lot of money. Roger, get your ass over here." Juan said, holding Nikki up.

Roger rushed over to Juan's side. He could tell Nikki was out of it. She was draped over Juan's arm. Nikki was murmuring but not making any sense. Her eyes were unfocused. Roger knew Juan had drugged her so Nikki could be transported to the auction without making a fuss.

Roger walked over to Juan. He picked Nikki up, cradling her in his arms, and carried her out of the room. Roger heard her mumble for help. Roger really wished he could help her and hoped Colin would be there to rescue her. Roger carried her to the waiting limo and bent down, putting her inside. Roger then climbed inside next to her. Roger whispered in her ear before anybody else got into the car.

"Nikki, Chance will be there tonight. Honey, he is here to take you home," Roger whispered.

"Chance....I want....Chance." Nikki mumbled.

"Shush, baby," Roger whispered.

"Chance...is ...that ...you?" Nikki cried. Juan climbed into the limo, sitting down across from Roger and Nikki.

"How's the money maker doing?" Juan asked, looking at Nikki with a smile.

"She is still out of it," Roger stated. Roger had his arm around her. Nikki had her head resting on his shoulder.

"Good, Nikki is going to bring in some serious money tonight. She is one sexy woman. My clients will be excited to see her."

"Yes, she is really sexy. I wish I could afford her," Roger started brushing a hand over her head on his shoulder.

"Damn, Roger, you have never been interested in any of the women. If I had known this, I would have let you try her out first before selling her?"

"How much do you want for her?" Roger asked. Juan stared at Roger in surprise.

"Are you serious, Roger? You really want her?"

"Yes, I am very serious."

"Well, you know she owes me $200,000.00, but I think I could get at least $700,000.00 for her at the auction," Juan stated. Roger sighed heavily. He shook his head.

"I am afraid that is more than I could afford," Roger said with disappointment. Juan laughed.

"Tell you what, Roger, if I don't get at least $200,000.00 for her, Nikki is yours for $50,000.00."

"Now, that price I can afford."

"Deal then. I will start the bidding at $50,000.00 for her. If I have no takers, Nikki is yours."

Roger nodded his head even though he knew Juan was lying to him. Juan would take no less than $200,000.00 for Nikki. Roger knew Nikki would see it at a high price. He hoped Colin had enough money to afford her. She would sell fast even though she wasn't as young as most of the girls.

Roger still couldn't figure out why those rich men liked the girls so young. He would rather have a woman with a woman's curves and experience. Roger wanted a woman who knew what the man wanted in bed. Instead of a girl who didn't know how to have good sex or please a man.

Chapter 17

Colin and Chance had been in Costa Rica for weeks without signs of Nikki. Colin had been in touch with Jackson, aka Roger. They were finally going to have the sex slave auction. Roger called Colin with the details and the invite pass they would need to get in. Jackson told Colin that Nikki would be there to be sold. Chance was fit to be tied. Chance paced the hotel room, pissed off.

“Chance, you need to calm down. We must keep our heads straight tonight.”

“I can’t believe that fucker. Juan has Nikki strung out on fucking drugs and now selling Nikki into sex slavery. The man is fucking animal. I want to fucking kill him.” Chance yelled in frustration.

"Chance, this is going to be hard on your tonight. You are going to restrain yourself and bite your fucking tongue. If you can’t do this, I will go by myself.”

“I fucking know that, Colin. I just don't like my hands being tied, knowing Nikki isn't that far away." Chance said, feeling frustrated and useless.

"You must brace yourself when Nikki is brought out on the auction block. You will have to hold yourself in check. Nikki will be put on display, naked or dressed. Men will be able to check and touch her if they are interested in purchasing her. Nikki is going to be one of many women for sale. There are going to be young girls, younger than Nikki also. Nikki is about 10 to 15 years older than the other girls for sale."

“Jeezus Colin!”

"I am telling you this so you are prepared for what you will see. It will shock the hell out of you to see how young some of the girls will be."

“Fuck! Will they be beaten and drugged up?"

"Most of the time. It is so the girls don't give the handlers any trouble."

"Shit, Colin! I feel sick."

“Chance, there is more you need to know.”

“What more?”

"I am posing as a sex slave buyer, which means we will have access to the women."

“Colin, what do you mean?”

“We will be able to view the women before they are on the auction stage.”

“Jeezus!”

"I will be able to go back to the cells where they keep the women. I am unsure if you will be allowed to come with me." Colin looked at Chance. Chance's face was paler as he felt sicker by the minute.

"If they allow you to come back with me, you must be prepared for what you see."

“Fuck!”

“The women will be in cells or cages. You will smell sweat, urine, vomit, and sex. They will be drugged up, naked or not. Some will be restrained. Some will come on to you or scream at you. The buyer can touch and sample the woman they are interested in."

Chance swallowed hard, trying to keep from vomiting. Colin reached out and squeezed his shoulder.

"Chance, I need to know you will be able to handle this and keep it together."

“Colin, I promise you, I will hold it together. We have to make sure you win the bid on Nikki.”

"I will not promise you that I will win the bid. But I will try my most damn to win, but I will not hesitate to knock you out cold if I have to.”

"I understand." Chance nodded his head in understanding. Colin squeezed Chance's shoulder again and stood up, leaving Chance to ponder what he had just told him.

Chance felt sick after talking to Colin. He knew this would be the hardest thing he had ever done. Chance was going to have to keep his emotions in check at all times. This would be the most challenging part to see Nikki drugged up and caged. Chance ran his hands through his hair in frustration.

It was around 9:00pm when Colin and Chance left for the auction. Colin had the directions to the warehouse where it was taking place. They arrived at the warehouse where the auction was being held. The warehouse was standing in a very isolated area. It had taken them more than a couple of hours to find it. There were a lot of expensive cars in the parking lot.

Chance and Colin climbed out of the rental car and walked to the door. Colin banged on the door. There was a slot in the door that opened. Colin held his phone to the niche so the person could see the invite and asked for the password.

"Dogs dance in the night," Colin stated. The door opened up. Chance and Colin walked inside the warehouse.

Chance was amazed. There had to be at least a hundred men mingling around and talking. He also noticed 70% of the men were foreigners. The men were all dressed in very expensive suits and looked like money. Chance and Colin approached the check-in desk. They were patted down for weapons and were checked for recording devices. They also had to show their identifications to ensure they were on the list of invites. Roger had made sure of it.

Chance and Colin moved into the next room. In the room, chairs were set up around the stage that was in the middle of the room. They were served expensive champagne or expensive wine. Chance looked around in amazement.

"Colin, do you recognize any of these men?" Chance asked quietly.

"Yes, remember to use Alex in case anyone overhears. I have seen a lot of them before. They are Stamos's best clients. They will spend a lot of money here tonight. Believe it or not, Juan will probably sell every one of the girls he has. I have heard his clients say Juan has the best selection of girls for sale. He doesn't keep them very long, just long enough to control them. He doesn't beat them into submission or let his keepers use them. Juan just drugs the girls to get them dependent on him until they are sold. Juan usually keeps them for a week or two, and that is it."

"What happens if he doesn't sell them?"

"Juan always sells all the girls. If they don't get sold, they will go up for prostitution."

"So, no matter what, their lives are doomed."

"Yes, it is. Sex slavery and prostitution have been going on since the beginning of time.

Unfortunately, it will never be stopped.

"It is unfair that women are treated like animals and possessions."

"You are right. It isn't fair, but unfortunately, it happens to young men also and all over the world."

Chapter 18

Juan, Roger, and Nikki arrived at the warehouse. Nikki was still out of it. Roger had to carry Nikki out of the limo into the warehouse. The warehouse had viewing rooms set up. Roger carried Nikki into one of the rooms. Juan had about 75 women here tonight to sell. Roger carefully laid Nikki on the bed. She moaned a little bit.

"Chance, please stay with me," Nikki mumbled. Roger sat down on the edge of the cot next to her. He brushed the hair off her face.

"Chance, please, I don't feel so well," Nikki mumbled. Roger knew this was the only chance he would have to talk to Nikki privately.

"Shush, Nikki, Chance is here to get you," Roger whispered next to her ear. Nikki tried to sit up. Roger helped her up. Nikki tried to focus her eyes to see where they were.

"Where is Chance. I don't see him. Chance, where are you? I can't see you," Nikki said, trying to focus on her eyes.

"Nikki, please. You need to listen to me." Roger said, trying to get her attention. He reached out, grabbed her chin, and turned her so she had to look at him.

"Where am I?" Nikki whispered, still feeling disoriented, staring at Roger. "Where is Chance?"

"Nikki, please; Chance isn't here right at the moment. You need to listen to me carefully."

" I don't like it here. I want to go home to Chance." Nikki cried, looking at Roger.

"I know. Please listen to me. Juan is gone right now, but he will be back shortly. So I don't have much time to explain shit to you." Roger stated. Nikki looked around the room. Nothing was in the room except for a single cot lying on the floor. The walls were gray and dingy looking. There were also bars on the doors like a jail cell. Nikki started to feel really uneasy.

"Where am I?" Nikki asked as the drug began wearing off more.

"Nikki, you need to listen to me carefully, please," Roger whispered. Nikki looked over at him, uneasy.

"Please, tell me where I am." Nikki slowly stood up unsteadily.

"Nikki, listen, you owe Juan a lot of money. He is going to collect on that debt tonight." Roger stated. Nikki looked at him and swallowed hard. Her hands twisted together uneasily.

"I figured that since I am all dressed in this sheer dressing gown," Nikki said, waving her hand down the gown.

"No, Nikki, you don't understand what I am trying to tell you. Juan is not going to have sex with you. You are here to be sold to the highest bidder." Roger whispered urgently. Nikki stared at him, confused.

"What do you mean?" Nikki asked nervously, looking at Roger wide-eyed and shaking her head in denial.

"Nikki, Juan is selling you tonight to the highest bidder. There are seventy-five women here this evening besides you. They are also being sold. You are going to be sold in a sex slave auction." Roger firmly stated.

Nikki was silent while she processed what Roger was telling her. Roger knew when she finally fully understood what was going to happen. A look of fear and disbelief crossed over her face.

"Oh my god!" Nikki cried, grabbing hold of Rogers's forearms. Her body started to shake uncontrollably. "Oh no, oh my god no, Roger, get me out of here, please," Nikki begged, squeezing his arms in desperation.

"Nikki, please, listen to me," Roger whispered, staring at her.

"Please, get me the fuck out of here!" Nikki sputtered.

Roger and Nikki heard the door unlock and open. Juan came into the room, smiling. Nikki pulled out of Roger's arms and ran over to Juan. She slapped Juan hard across the face before Roger could catch her.

"You rotten son of bitch!" Nikki yelled, trying to slap Juan again.

"You fucking bitch," Juan backhanded her across the face before she could slap him again. Nikki fell into Roger from the blow to her face. Roger caught Nikki before she hit the ground. Roger wrapped his arms around her waist. Nikki struggled against Roger as Juan moved closer to her. Juan grabbed her jaw in a punishing grip holding on tightly, staring into her fear-filled eyes.

"You listen to me, you little whore! You owe me a lot of money, and I intend to collect it. You are going to pay me back tonight!" Juan yelled in anger.

Nikki shrugged out of Rogers's grip. She was pissed off and scared. Nikki straightened herself back up, then stood before Juan with hate-filled eyes even as her body trembled with fear.

"I am not a fucking whore. I owe and operate a respectable business that you took advantage of. I respected you and your family; never once did I disrespect any of you. You are a piece of shit. You can't treat me like this."

"The fuck I can't. You are now my fucking bitch. I will sell to the highest bidder tonight, and there is not a fucking thing you can do about it. I now own you." Juan yelled.

Nikki moved to hit him again, and Juan caught her hand before it connected with his face; Juan bent her hand backward. Nikki cried out in pain. Juan kept turning her hand back until Nikki knelt on the floor before him.

"See bitch, you are where you belong, kneeling before me. You listen to me carefully. You have no life now. Your life will be to please the man who buys you. You are never going home," Juan sneered at her disgustingly.

"Roger, give this bitch some coke to shut her up. That will settle her ass down. I don't want her to attack any potential buyers."

"No! I don't want any more of your fucking drugs," Nikki yelled. Juan applied more pressure to her hand. Nikki cried out in pain again.

"Roger, give her the fucking shot, now!" Juan stated firmly.

"Okay, boss," Roger said, nodding his head. Juan pulled a vial out of his pocket and handed it to Roger. Nikki looked at Roger with pleading eyes. Roger plunged the needle into her arm. Roger didn't give her all of it.

Roger hoped that Juan didn't notice. Juan let go of Nikki's hand. Roger recapped the needle and put it into his pocket. Juan walked to the door and then stopped.

"I need you to check on the other women. Make sure everything is all set for the auction. The auction will begin within half an hour." Juan stated, then walked out of the room, closing the door behind him.

Nikki sat on the floor. She started to feel the drug rushing through her system. Her heart rate began to speed up, and she felt lightheaded. Roger tried to help her off the floor, but Nikki swatted his hand away. She slowly got up off the floor and sat down on the cot.

"Nikki, you need to keep yourself calm and level-headed," Roger stated.

"Fuck you, just leave me the fuck alone," Nikki replied.

"I didn't give you the whole vial. it will wear off in a few hours." Roger said.

"Just fucking leave me alone."

Roger turned and walked to the door. He turned back and looked at Nikki with sorrow in his eyes, knowing he had to leave. Roger couldn't help Nikki without blowing his cover. He sighed heavily and walked out the door, knowing there was nothing more he could do for her. Roger could not blow his cover for Nikki.

Nikki heard the door close and lock after Roger left the room. She felt numb inside. Tears slowly started rolling down her face. She listened to the cries of the other women in their cells like hers. Nikki knew she was in big trouble. Her mind was too fuzzy to think about the predicament she was in. Nikki curled up on the cot in a fetal position.

Chapter 19

Chance and Colin walked around the building, checking the place out. Colin spotted Juan Stamos laughing and walking around, talking to some buyers. Colin slapped Chance on the back.

"Juan Stamos just entered the room," Colin whispered next to Chance.

"Point him out to me," Chance said, turning around. Colin pointed Juan out. Juan was talking to some buyers across the room from them. Juan excused himself from the group and walked onto the stage.

"Excuse me, gentlemen," Juan said. Everybody was quiet, with their attention on Juan.

"First, I would like to thank everybody for coming. I am positive everyone will be pleased with the goods for sale tonight. Everyone will have the opportunity to go back in groups of ten to look at the merchandise for sale. If you want to look closer at the goods, just tell one of the handlers. The handler will then let you into the room for a closer look. Thank you, gentlemen. I hope you find the goods to your liking," Juan said, smiling.

"I have never hated a man more than I do right now," Chance said between clenched teeth.

"Okay, Chance, now is the time to keep your cool. Jackson just texted my phone a little while ago. Nikki is here and will be the last on the block." Colin stated.

"I will hold it together, but I want to kill that mother fucker with my bare hands."

"I understand but put that thought out of your head. Juan and Joseph Stamos are untouchable right now."

"I will hold it together, but it doesn't mean I cannot think of hundred different ways to kill Juan in my mind."

"Hold your emotions in check. What is coming up next will be gut retching. Let's get ready to get into the lineup," Colin said, studying Chance for any apprehension.

"As ready as I will ever be," Chance replied, taking a deep breath. He noticed Juan Stamos was walking towards them. Chance nudged Colin with his arm.

"Juan is walking this way," Chance whispered softly. Colin turned and smiled at Juan approaching them.

"Mr. Stamos, you have a great turnout tonight," Colin said, holding his hand out to Juan. Juan shook his hand, eyeballing Chance.

"Mr. Malcolm, great to see you again. It has been a couple of years since the last time. Who is this with you?" Juan asked curiously.

"Mr. Stamos, this is my brother Daniel. He is looking for something," Colin replied.

"Nice to meet you, Daniel. Are you looking for something to keep your bed warm at night or something to play with?" Juan asked curiously, holding out his hand to Chance. Chance would have rather squeezed until Juan screamed in pain than shake the slim ball's hand.

"I am looking for something warm with a little bit of sass," Chance stated, smiling. Juan laughed.

"You are interested in a sex slave?" Juan asked.

"If I find one that appeals to me. I will be very interested." Chance said.

"Something with sass, then make sure you check out the last room," Juan stated.

'Does the merchandise still have sass and spirit left?" Chance asked.

"Just check out the last room. You will find it to your liking. What are you looking for, Mr. Alex?"

"I am keeping my options open," Colin stated.

"I am something for everybody's taste. Happy shopping, gentleman." Juan said, smiling, then walked away from them. Chance let out a sigh of relief.

"Do you think that son of a bitch was referring to Nikki?" Chance asked through gritted teeth.

"Yes, Roger said Nikki was the last to be brought in."

Chance noticed another man approaching them. Jake Rollins saw Colin Black was here. Jake recognized Colin through his disguise. Jake and Colin had worked together for two years trying to find Congressman Collins's daughter Camille.

Jake slowly approached Colin. Jake wondered why Colin was here now and in disguise. Colin was no longer in the Marines and shouldn't be here.

"Alex Malcolm, what the hell are you doing here?" Jake asked, puzzled. Colin smiled at Jake, holding out his hand. Jake grabbed Colin's and shook it firmly.

"Jake, it is great to see you again. This is my brother, Daniel Malcolm," Colin replied, smiling. Colin could see the questions in Jake's eyes. Jake nodded at Chance and shook his hand. Jake quickly glanced around to ensure no one was close enough to hear him question Colin.

"Colin, what the fuck are you doing here?" Jake whispered.

"Friend of Chance's is here. She is being sold tonight." Colin said softly.

"How the fuck did you get in here?" Jake asked.

"Jackson Adams, aka Roger Belford. I had him as a contact from the previous job, so I contacted him about Chance's friend, Nikki Curtis. Nikki has been flying shipments for the Stamos family for six months now. She had no idea that she was transporting drugs instead of goods. Last week one of the containers broke open in her plane from a storm. She panicked and threw the container away. Evidently, there was $200,000.00 worth of cocaine pitched in the trash. So least to say, the Stamos family was not impressed. So this is Juan's idea of getting his money back."

"Holy fuck! Show me which woman, and I will help you get her back. We are still looking for Camille Collins. We are hoping she is here tonight." Jake stated.

"Thank you, Jake; I will owe you one," Colin replied.

"Yes, you will; believe me, I will come and collect," Jake stated firmly. Colin laughed. The three of them went over to the line. Jake glanced at Chance. Jake could see the tension lines and tension in Chance's body language.

"Your brother has never done this before," Jake said softly to Colin.

"No, he hasn't. He will be fine," Colin said, looking at Chance.

"I hope so for your sake," Jake stated.

"He will do fine. If not, I will have to knock his ass out cold," Colin stated firmly. Jake nodded his head in agreement.

As the three entered the sale block, the smell of sex, urine, and sweat hit their noses. Chance thought he was going to vomit. Chance's breath started to come out more quickly as he tried not to take deep breaths. Colin noticed Chance's breathing had picked up, and he winced. Colin cleared his throat, staring straight at Chance. Chance raised his hand, letting Colin know he was alright. Colin patted him on the arm. They moved inside the block further.

The warehouse had rooms set up like a jail. The women were in cells with bars on the top portion of the door and solid steel below. The doors were numbered so the buyers could write the number down if they wanted to bid on the woman.

At the first cell, Chance was surprised at how young the girl was. She couldn't have been older than 16. She was a beautiful Oriental girl with long black hair that hung to her butt. She was dressed in a sheer red lingerie teddy with red stiletto heels. The young girl smiled at them and started dancing seductively. She didn't seem to care that the men were watching her. Her eyes were glassy from being drugged up. The young girl twirled in circles showing herself off to the men watching and then blowing kisses.

"Holy fuck!" Chance muttered under his breath, watching the young girl.

"Be easy, brother. This is only the first one." Colin stated.

The young girl moved closer to the door staring at them. She raised her hand, pushing her top to the side, running her hand over her small breasts, then pinching and twisting her nipples.

"Pick me; I can please you," The girl smiled, cupping her breasts, then running her hand down between her legs, cupping her pussy.

"She is too fucking young to be acting like a whore," Chance whispered, feeling sick looking at the young girl.

Colin turned his head, staring at Chance with a stern look. Chance nodded his head in understanding to shut his mouth. They moved to the next room. Chance couldn't believe how young most of the women were.

Actually, they weren't even women yet; they were young girls. Every one of the girls was dressed in sexy lingerie and drugged. Some of them seemed to be enjoying the show, and some were scared as hell. They finally made it towards the end. All the men appeared to be grouped in the last room. Chance then heard Nikki's voice. His heart raced faster with the urge to go to Nikki quickly. Colin reached out and squeezed Chance's arm.

"What the fuck are you all looking at, assholes," Nikki screamed. "Get the hell out of here. You will never fucking touch me!" Chance's face was pale, and he was breathing hard, hearing Nikki scream.

"Be easy, Daniel," Colin replied, gripping Chance's arm firmer. "You will not be helping her if you lose your shit now." Chance nodded his head and tried to get his breathing under control. Jake glanced at them.

"Is that her?" Jake asked quietly. Colin nodded his head. They moved forward to the last room. Jake, Colin, and Chance looked inside the room. Chance felt like he would be sick seeing Nikki inside the room.

Nikki was dressed in a long white sheer dressing gown. Her body was visible through the material. Her hair and makeup were done to perfection. Nikki's eyes were bright, and their complexion was flushed with anger.

Chance was surprised at how beautiful Nikki looked. He was not expecting to see her looking like a sex goddess. Chance did notice the darkness around her jaw area where there had been bruises that were fading. He felt anger run through his body, knowing that son of a bitch Stamos put the bruise there.

Nikki was pacing the room in anger and fear. She felt like a zoo animal being looked at. The men were all leering at her. Nikki turned her back to them and spit at the window. Colin approached the handler.

"I want a closer look at the woman," Colin stated firmly.

"Just you?" The handler asked.

"I and my brother," Colin said, waving his hand at Chance. The handler nodded his head and unlocked the door.

"Are you sure? This one is fit to be tied right now. She has been hitting and kicking at other buyers." The handler stated.

"I like my woman with a little sass," Colin stated.

The handler nodded his head and let them inside the room. Colin and Chance entered the room. Nikki suddenly turned around quickly. Nikki ran at Colin with her fists clenched. She moved fast, throwing punches at Colin. Colin tried to grab her fists. She screamed, then started to kick and punch him.

"Get the fuck away from me, you fucker!" Nikki screamed, punching Colin in the ribs.

Colin grunted out as her punch landed in his rib cage. Colin grabbed hold of her fists. He bent her hand back until she whimpered in pain.

"Get on your fucking knees, bitch," Colin sneered, twisting her hand back until Nikki was on her knees before him. Chance felt the urge to punch his brother for hurting Nikki.

"What the fuck?" Chance whispered out to his brother between clenched teeth.

"You will fucking submit to me," Colin stated firmly, staring at Nikki before him, bending her hand more.

"I will never fucking submit to any man, asshole!" Nikki said between clenched teeth as more pain raced through her hand.

Nikki glanced over at Chance. She, of course, didn't recognize him at all. Nikki could see the pain in his eyes, like he felt sorry for her. Colin still had a hold of her hand, bending it backward. Tears formed in her eyes from the pain. Chance knelt down beside her. Nikki spat in his face. Chance wiped the spit off his face.

"Nikki," Chance whispered softly.

Nikki looked at the man with puzzlement. How did he know her name? She stared at him with confusion when Chance bent down closer to her. Chance put his head down next to her ear. Nikki tried to hit Chance with her other hand, but Colin applied more pressure to her hand. Nikki cried out in pain.

"Don't you dare," Colin stated firmly.

"Get the fuck away from me!" Nikki yelled.

"Nikki, stop it. I am here," Chance whispered softly to her.

Nikki was started by the man's voice. She knew that voice, but this man was not Chance. The man sounded like Chance but didn't look anything like him. The drugs were playing tricks on her mind. Chance knew Nikki didn't recognize him at all. He decided not to push the issue since he could see the needle marks on her arms.

"Please, don't fucking touch me," Nikki begged. Chance nodded his head, standing up and looking at Colin. Colin gave Chance a firm look. Chance knew he had to be careful. Colin released Nikki's hand. She rubbed her wrist. Nikki sat on the floor glaring at Chance and Colin angrily, then spat at them. Colin laughed at her and left the room, with Chance following behind. Chance looked at Nikki one last time before the door closed.

"Well done, brother," Colin said, relaxing a little as they walked away.

Chance didn't say a word, still shocked at seeing Nikki here. Nikki was dressed in a sexy sheer dressing gown. Chance knew Juan had kept Nikki drugged up by the needle marks on her arms. Nikki's eyes were dilated and wild looking. Her body was twitching with the need for more drugs. She had dark circles under her eyes like she hadn't slept in a week. She was also sniffing a lot and rubbing her nose. Chance could see Nikki had lost weight.

Jake, Colin, and Chance walked back out to the stage area. They were handed more champagne. They made their way to some seats and sat down. Colin looked over at Chance with concern.

"You okay?" Colin asked softly.

"Yes," Chance said, taking a sip of the champagne. " I can't believe Nikki didn't recognize my voice."

"Probably the drugs," Colin replied.

"They have been pumping Nikki full of drugs. I saw the needle marks in her arms." Chance said.

"The auction will be starting soon. I don't want you to freak out, but I will have to bid on a few girls so there is no suspicion." Colin said. Chance nodded his head.

"What happens if you win the bid?" Chance asked.

"We take them with us," Colin said. Jake sat down next to Colin. "Jake, I might need your help. I only have $100,000.00. I have a feeling Nikki is going for a hell of a lot more than I have," Colin said quietly so Chance couldn't hear him.

"Don't worry. I have your back. Nikki will be leaving with you. I promise." Jake stated firmly.

"Thank you," Colin said.

"Oh, you will pay me back," Jake stated.

"Yes, so you have told me a few times," Colin laughed.

"I hope she goes for more. I could really use your help," Jake said.

"You will have it," Colin replied.

Nikki sat on the bed, trembling in fear. She watched the young girls being led out of the rooms one by one. Some made a fuss, and some just walked silently in a daze. Nikki was surprised at how young most of the girls were. Some of the girls weren't even 18 years old yet.

Nikki felt sick for the young girls and the parents that had lost them to sex trafficking. The young girls were too young to even experience sex yet. Nikki couldn't believe men would even want a girl that young, the sick fucking bastards.

The girls had to be more frightened than she was. Nikki knew what those sick bastards wanted from the young girls. They wanted to train them to be sex slaves. The bastards would use and abuse them to get what they wanted. Once the bastards were done with the girls, they would throw them away like trash. Most of the girls then would turn to prostitution.

Nikki was afraid for herself too. She could end up in a foreign country with no way of getting back home. She was already craving the coke that Juan got her hooked on. Nikki was shaking from the need for the drug. The more she thought of the coke, panic, and anxiety started to settle over her. She began to pace the room, wringing her hands. Nikki felt like her skin was crawling all over, making her twitchy. She needed the coke terribly now. Her mouth was dry, and her head began to hurt.

Nikki looked out the door, hoping to see Juan or Roger. She didn't see either. Nikki rubbed her aching temples as she began to pace every square inch of the room. Nikki tried to picture Chance in her mind, and the fun they had together in and out of bed, but the craving for the coke was stronger. Her mind would go back to when Juan or Roger would come back into the room to get her a fix. She chewed on her bottom lip, leaving indents on her teeth.

Nikki couldn't chew on her fingernails anymore because she chewed the nails too short. Nikki walked faster around the room, rubbing her arms. Nothing was helping; she felt like screaming and pulling her hair out. She heard Roger's voice down the hallway. Nikki quickly went to the door.

"Roger!" Nikki yelled out. "Roger, please help me." Nikki waved her hand between the bars, hoping Roger would see it.

Roger heard his name being yelled out. He looked down the hallway and saw a hand waving between the bars. Roger knew it was Nikki's room. He looked around for Juan and saw him by the stage area. Roger quickly rushed down to Nikki's room.

"Roger, please. I need a fix, please," Nikki begged through the door seeing Roger at the door. Roger unlocked the door and then quickly shut the door.

"Nikki, are you sure you want the rest?" Roger asked softly. Nikki nodded her head vigorously, feeling the excitement.

"Yes, please. I feel like I am crawling out of my skin," Nikki said, licking her lips and seeing Roger pull the vial from his pocket.

"Okay, give me your arm," Roger said. Nikki quickly gave him her arm. Roger took the cap off the needle and plunged it into her arm.

"Thank you," Nikki said with relief.

"You need to keep your head level. The handler will take you out on the auction block soon." Roger stated, pulling the needle out of her arm.

"They will have to kill me first. I will not be sold like an animal. I will fight with everything inside of me before any of them fuckers will touch me." Nikki stated firmly.

"Nikki, Chance..." Roger didn't get to finish. The handler was at the door looking inside.

"Hey, man, what the fuck are you doing in there?" The handler asked, glaring at Roger.

"I work for Juan, so watch your fucking tone with me. I was giving her some more arm candy," Roger stated firmly, showing the handler the vial.

"Sorry man, I thought maybe you were trying to sample the goods," The handler said.

"You are fucking wrong," Roger stated, opening the door and walking out.

"Sorry," The handler said, locking the door behind Roger.

Nikki sat down on the cot. She sighed in relief, feeling the cocaine run through her system. Her body stopped twitching, and her skin felt normal again. She laid back on the cot, staring up at the ceiling with a smile.

Chapter 20

The auction began; Chance sat on the edge of his seat, unsure what to expect. The first young girl was brought out by her handler. She had a collar around her neck with a leash hooked so the girl couldn't escape her handler. The young girl couldn't be more than 20 years old. She looked to be Oriental. She had long, straight black hair that hung down her back to her butt. The young girl was very petite and dressed in a sheer red teddy.

The young girl stood on the stage, looking out at the crowd with fear. The handler stood next to her. The bids began at $5,000 and then began to rise. The handler made the young girl turn in circles so the crowd could see all of her. Once the bidding rose to $30,000, the crowd began to yell orders to see more of the girl.

"Jeezus!" Chance muttered in disgust, hearing the men yell to undress the girl. "Are they really going to undress the poor girl?" Colin nodded his head.

"Yes. The clients want to see all of her before making the purchase," Colin said softly.

"I am so disgusted," Chance replied.

"It is very degrading," Colin said.

The handler removed the girl's clothes. The poor girl stood still on the stage naked. She was visibly shaking, tears rolling down her cheeks, dripping off her chin. The crowd didn't even care that the poor was scared to death.

Chance felt sick and couldn't even look at the stage. He wanted to rush down to the stage and cover the poor girl. The men were making disgusting remarks. He heard the bidding go up to $100,000 for the girl when the girl was sold. Chance thought he would vomit seeing the man cheer that had bought her. He stood up and bowed to the crowd. The man had to be in his late 40s.

Chance wanted to rush over to the man and beat the shit out of him for being a sick bastard. He couldn't understand what the men saw in the girls that were so young. The girls were young enough to be every one of those men's daughters. At 32, Chance was old enough to be the girl's father. Chance was sick and angry watching more young girls being brought out on stage, and the process was repeated.

Colin glanced over at Chance with concern. He could tell this whole thing was making Chance sick and angry. Colin grew concerned.

"Are you doing alright," Colin asked, concerned.

"This is so fucking sick," Chance whispered.

"I know. I am going to start bidding a little bit. Juan is watching the whole crowd to see who is bidding." Colin stated. Chance nodded his head.

"I don't have to like it," Chance replied.

"You are correct, but I don't want Juan to be suspicious of us being here. So, I have to bid on a few."

Colin and Jake began to bid on girls. Chance was not too happy watching his brother and Jake bid on girls. Thank god Colin didn't win the bids. But then Chance was worried about what would happen to the girls. He was torn by his feelings of relief and guilt. Chance knew Colin would release the girls and find their families. But what would happen to the girls if they had no family or a family that didn't care. Chance heard Juan announce there were ten more women to go. Chance started to feel anxious and nervous for Nikki.

Nikki still didn't know he was here for her. She had not recognized him earlier when he and Colin were in her cell. Chance was glad Nikki had not but was disappointed that she didn't either.

This set of women was a little older. The women at least looked over 18. Chance silently watched the women being sold one by one. Chance started to worry because Nikki had not come out yet. Juan strolled out on the stage. He smiled at the audience.

"Gentlemen, we have one more woman to be sold. The bidding for this woman will start at $100,000.00. If you are unwilling to pay that much for a very high-spirited woman of 25, you can leave," Juan announced. He waited on the stage and watched some of the men get up to leave. There were about 40 men left for the bidding. Juan laughed as the screams of a woman could be heard.

"Get your fucking hands off me!" Nikki screamed at the handlers. Two men had to forcefully take Nikki to the auction stage. Nikki struggled against them, but the handlers gripped her arms tighter. Nikki tried to hit, bit, and kick them as they dragged her onto the stage.

"You fuckers let go of me!" Nikki yelled.

Juan stood on the stage smiling as the men pulled Nikki onto the stage. The handlers let go of Nikki and pushed her at Juan. Juan gripped her by the arm tightly. Nikki tried to slap and kick him.

"Let go of me!" Nikki yelled and spit at Juan. Juan backhanded her across the face.

Nikki fell to the floor from the blow to the face. Juan grabbed her hand, bending it backward. Nikki cried out in pain as she quickly knelt in front of Juan. Juan looked out at the audience with a smile.

"I told you this woman had spirit. This is the one for you if you want a woman who will fight you at every turn. She will be a lot of fun to break and tame. Just think of the fun you will have in bed with this little spitfire," Juan announced, laughing, looking down at Nikki before him.

"You can't do this to me," Nikki said between clenched teeth.

"Oh, but I can. You will sell for a lot of money. You just keep putting a show on for the men, and the price will climb higher," Juan stated.

Chance silently cheered Nikki on. She hadn't lost her spirit. When Juan backhanded Nikki across the face, Chance rose up from his seat, feeling his blood boil in anger. Colin's hand swung out instantly and forcefully pushed Chance back down in his seat with a stern stare.

"Don't even think about it. You need to stay calm. So sit your fucking ass back down now. I can knock your ass out standing up," Colin stated firmly. Chance glanced at Colin's face. Colin was so calm, but his eyes were filled with anger.

"You need to keep it together because I am not kidding about knocking your ass out cold," Colin stated. Chance nodded his head, understanding.

"Is everything okay with you two?" Jake asked, concerned.

"Yep, we are fine for now," Colin stated. Jake nodded his head and glanced over at Chance. They made eye contact, and Chance nodded his head. Jake turned his attention back to the stage.

"How much do you think Nikki is going to go for?" Colin asked Jake.

"I am not sure, but I think it is going to go high," Jake replied.

"Fuck! That is what I was afraid of," Colin muttered.

"No worries, I got you covered," Jake replied. Colin nodded his head.

Nikki tried to hit Juan with her other hand. But Juan, of course, applied pressure to the hand he was holding.

"You son of a bitch!" Nikki cried out in pain, then spit at Juan again. Juan looked down at her and then slapped Nikki across the face again.

"Well, gentlemen, I was not kidding about this high-spirited one. It will be a fun challenge to break her. The bidding on this little gem will start at $100,000," Juan laughed.

As the bidding began, two handlers picked Nikki up off the floor. One pulled her arms behind her back, holding them firmly. Nikki struggled against the handler, trying to kick and bit the second one. She was not giving up the fight.

The bidding grew higher. The second handler reached out and untied Nikki's dressing gown. He pulled the sheer material aside, exposing her naked body. The handlers showed Nikki off like an animal for purchase. The handler tried to pry her mouth open to show off her teeth. Nikki, of course, tried to bite the handler.

Chance had to clench his jaw tightly, growling his displeasure watching the scene on the stage. Chance knew he could do nothing except watch like everyone else around them did. Chance also knew Colin was keeping a close eye on him.

Nikki kept struggling against the men holding her even though it didn't do any good. Chance noticed Colin had stopped bidding on her. The bidding was up to $350,000.

"Why the fuck did you stop bidding?" Chance growled with anger.

"I don't have enough money to go any higher. Don't worry; Jake is bidding on Nikki for us," Colin stated.

"Colin, what the fuck," Chance hissed angrily.

"Just be quiet and trust me with this. Nikki will be leaving with you tonight," Colin said firmly.

"You better be right, Colin, or I can guarantee shit will hit the fan, and it will not be in a good way," Chance growled.

The bidding was now at $500,000. Jake glanced at Colin. Colin nodded his head for Jake to keep bidding. Jake raised his hand to accept the price. A few minutes later, the bidding jumped to $600,000. There were only four men besides Jake left in the bidding war.

The rest of the men started to leave. Juan waited for several minutes before beginning the bidding again. Chance was feeling anxious and nervous watching the other four men that were left. He wished they would give up and leave. Chance wanted to rush down to the stage and grab Nikki and go.

"Jake can't lose the bid, Colin," Chance whispered in concern, feeling sick.

"Relax," Colin stated, staring at Chance with intensity. Chance nodded his head.

The bidding was now up to $800,000. Again Jake glanced over at Colin. Colin nodded his head for Jake to keep going.

"You are mine, Alex," Jake said, smiling.

What does Jake mean by that comment?" Chance asked, concerned for Colin.

"Don't worry; everything is fine," Colin replied harshly.

"Tell me what Jake means," Chance stated.

"Later, now shut up," Colin growled.

The bid was now $850,000. Jake and another man were the only two left. The man bidding against Jake was Arab. The Arab kept looking over at Jake with his black eyes to see if Jake was still bidding. The bid climbed to $900,000. The Arab looked at Jake, nodded his head, then stood up, shaking his head at Juan, letting him know he was now finished bidding. Chance watched the man get up and leave. Chance felt excitement run through his body.

"Holy shit! Did Jake win the bid?" Chance asked nervously.

"Yes," Colin said calmly.

"It is over; Nikki is mine?" Chanced asked, holding his breath.

"Yes, Nikki is coming with us. Now calm down," Colin stated firmly. Chance swallowed down his excitement.

"We need to leave. Jake will bring Nikki to us at the airport. You and Nikki will fly out of here tonight immediately." Colin stated firmly.

Colin stood up, reaching out to shake Jake's hand. Colin started to walk in the opposite direction from Jake. Chance followed Colin with confusion. Chance didn't want to leave without Nikki. Colin walked out of the warehouse with Chance trailing behind him. Chance was beginning to feel anger rise inside of him. Chance stopped walking. Colin turned around to look at him.

"What the fuck, Colin?" Chance barked.

"Just get into the fucking car, Chance," Colin stated, pointing at the car. Chance looked back at the warehouse. The urge to go back inside to get Nikki was overwhelming. Chance began to walk towards the warehouse, not wanting to leave without Nikki.

"Chance, get into the fucking car, NOW!" Colin barked in anger, grabbing hold of Chance's arm.

"Get the fuck off me, Colin," Chance yelled, pulling his arm from Colin's grip.

"I am warning you, Chance. I will fucking knock your ass out if you don't get inside the fucking car, NOW!" Colin warned. Chance pulled his arm from Colin's grip taking a few steps back.

Chance stared at his younger brother. Colin stared at him with anger and determination. Chance knew there would be a fight if he didn't get into the car. Colin started walking towards him aggressively. Colin stopped directly in front of Chance.

"Chance, if you want to see Nikki alive, get the fuck into the car. You are going to get Nikki. If you don't get into the car, Jake and we will get hurt or killed."

"You promise Jake will bring Nikki to the airport?" Chance asked.

"On my life, Jake will bring Nikki to the airport, promise," Colin stated.

Chance knew Colin was not lying to him. Chance nodded his head, walking towards the car. They both climbed inside the car. Colin started driving away. Chance tensed up as he watched the warehouse disappear in the side mirror. Colin reached over, patting Chance on the arm.

"Chance, I promise everything will be okay. Jake will bring Nikki to the airport. You need to make arrangements to fly out immediately."

"What about you?" Chance asked. Colin looked over at him.

"I am staying here," Colin replied.

"What the fuck, do you mean?" Chance yelled with concern.

"I will call Carter and explain everything to him. I don't have time to get into the details with you. As soon as Jake shows up with Nikki, you must fly out immediately."

"Colin, what's happening now?"

"Nikki will have to change her life. She can't go back to her flying business. Hector will know her. She will have to start her life all over again in a new state. The further away from Hector Stamos and his sons, the better. Nikki will be on the run until they are brought down."

Chance was startled by Colin's comment. He hadn't thought of Nikki still being in danger from Hector Stamos once they got her out of the sex slave ring.

"Fuck, Colin, I didn't think of that," Chance stated.

"Chance, you must ensure Nikki understands her life is done here. If Hector Stamos sees Nikki, she is a dead woman. Nikki will need to move as soon as possible. If you love her, you will have to decide if you will move. Both of your lives will change forever after tonight." Colin stated firmly. Chance nodded his head in agreement. They were silent for a few minutes.

"Colin, thank you for helping me get Nikki," Chance said, glancing at his brother. Colin looked over at Chance with a smile.

"That is what brothers are for."

"You acted like an older brother tonight instead of me and made me keep my cool."

"If the tables were turned, you would have done the same for me."

"Yes, I would have without hesitation," Chance punched Colin in the arm.

Colin and Chance arrived at the hotel at 1:00am. They walked up to the room. Chance started packing his luggage, then called the airport and told them he would be leaving tonight.

Chapter 21

Nikki was led back to the room where she was before the auction. She felt numb inside and made her mind blank. Nikki didn't want to think about what was going to happen now. She sat down on the bed. She felt so empty inside and couldn't even cry. Nikki realized her life was gone. She was never going to see or hold Chance again.

The handler stood next to her, holding a needle in his hand. Nikki held out her arm to him. She didn't care right now and wanted to forget what happened briefly. Nikki felt the needle plunge into her arm. The handler left the room after giving her the shot.

Nikki felt the rush of the drug through her system and welcomed it. She lay down on the bed in a drug-induced haze. Nikki saw a strange man enter the room and didn't even care. The stranger pulled her up to her feet.

"Come with me," the man said softly, putting his arm around her waist.

Nikki tried to stand up and follow him. The man put her arm around his neck and then had to hold her up by the waist. Jake made his way to the door, with Nikki knowing she was drugged up. Jake was thankful because Nikki wasn't fighting him.

Jake and Nikki made their way out of the room. Jake decided it would be easier to carry Nikki instead of half-carrying and dragging her. Jake bent down and picked Nikki up. He carried Nikki out fireman style over his shoulder. Nikki didn't even struggle against him as he carried her out of the warehouse.

Jake was almost out of the car when Roger approached him and Nikki. Roger smiled at Jake and opened the car door for Jake. Jake put Nikki into the back seat of the car.

"Thank you," Jake said, looking at Roger.

"Take care of her. Nikki didn't belong in there," Roger whispered.

"Um...I will," Jake replied, puzzled.

"Tell Colin to get Nikki far away from Hector, or she is dead," Roger stated. Jake stared at him with confusion.

"I am not the enemy. I am on your side. I have been uncovering for three years now. Jackson Adams, aka Roger Belford, I am with the FBI. Here is my private number," Roger replied and walked away.

Jake was stunned at his comment. Jake climbed into the car and drove away with Nikki safely inside. He was to meet Colin at the hotel. Jake called Colin.

"Jake, are you all right?" Colin asked quickly.

"Yes, I have Nikki, Colin. She is drugged up. I can't take her to the hotel. It would draw attention to us." Jake stated.

"I figured that. So meet up at the airport. Chance already called and informed them he was leaving tonight. As soon as you get here, Chance will be leaving with Nikki immediately," Colin replied.

"All right, I will see you there," Jake said. Colin hung up his phone. Chance carried his luggage and Nikki's luggage to the door setting it down.

"Who called?" Chance asked.

"Jake, we have to meet him at the airport. Nikki has been drugged again. Jake didn't want to draw attention by bringing her to the hotel."

"Okay, I am all set," Chance stated.

"Let's go then," Colin replied.

Chance grabbed his luggage, and Nikki's out the door. Colin and Chance checked out of the hotel and walked down to the car. Chance loaded the luggage. They climbed into the car and headed to the airport. Colin drove to slot 21, where the airplane was waiting. Chance and Colin loaded the luggage into the plane. Chance quickly did a pre-flight check.

Chance climbed into the plane's cockpit and radioed the tower, letting them know he would be ready to leave within the hour. Colin spotted a car heading their way. He watched it slowly approach. Colin hoped it was Jake but was unsure if it was. The car pulled up to the plane. It was a black Mercedes Benz. Colin quickly dialed Jake's number.

"Colin, what's up?" Jake asked.

"Are you in a black Mercedes Benz?" Colin asked.

"No, I am just entering the airport in a gray Lincoln town car," Jake replied.

"Stay back; I am unsure who this is in the Mercedes."

"Call me back when it is clear," Jake stated. Colin hung up his phone.

"Chance, we have company, be alert," Colin said as Chance climbed out of the plane. Chance looked over Colin's shoulder, seeing the car sitting a few feet away.

"Who do you think it is?" Chance asked, concerned.

"Not sure, but be ready for anything," Colin stated.

The doors on the car opened up. Roger and Juan climbed out of the car. They walked towards Chance and Colin.

"What the fuck!" Chance whispered.

"Stay calm," Colin whispered back.

"Mr. Stamos, what brings you out here?" Colin asked, holding out his hand. Juan walked up and shook his hand.

"You and your brother left empty-handed. So, I was concerned. Did you not find my goods to your taste, Alex?" Juan asked, smiling.

"Your goods were excellent. My brother was interested in the last woman, but we lost the bid." Colin stated.

"Yes, she was definitely a high-spirited woman. She attracted a lot of attention and sold for a terrific price. But you didn't find anything to your taste?" Juan stated.

"I did but was out bided each time. I guess it wasn't my lucky night. Daniel is getting ready to fly out tonight. He is needed back in the States. I am staying for a while. Will there be another auction?" Colin asked.

"Yes, there will be another auction in a week or two. Maybe you will find someone more to your liking." Juan replied.

"I hope so. Please make sure I am on your invite list. I will definitely be there."

"I have a business proposal for you. I think you might be interested in it. Would you meet me for dinner tomorrow night?" Juan asked.

"You have a business proposal for me, interesting. You have my curiosity peaked. I would be glad to meet you."

"Great, I will see you tomorrow night. Daniel, it was a pleasure to meet you. I hope I will meet again." Juan said, holding out his hand to Chance. Chance shook his hand.

"I wish I could stay longer for the next auction, thank you. I really enjoyed it," Chance said, smiling feeling his stomach clench in disgust and swallowing the bile that rose up in his throat.

Juan nodded his head, then turned, walking back to the car. Roger followed him. Chance and Colin watched them climb back into the car.

"Jeezus, I thought I was going to vomit," Chance stated. "What was that all about?"

"I am not sure. But I will discuss it with Jake." Colin stated, then called Jake. " The coast is clear."

About fifteen minutes later, Jake pulled up next to the plane. Chance's heart was racing with excitement and anxiety to see Nikki. Colin grabbed his arm.

"Chance, Nikki is drugged up. You will have to be gentle with her. Nikki will not recognize you in your disguise," Colin cautioned.

"Shit, I forgot I still had on this disguise."

"Just remember, Nikki, is going to be disoriented and confused. Roger said Juan has her hooked on coke. So you will have that to deal with also." Colin stated. Chance nodded his head, understanding. Jake walked towards them. He did not look happy with a grim expression.

"I must warn you before you get Nikki out of the car. I had to tie her up. Nikki is pissed off right now. Halfway there, she got her spirit back. I had to pull off the road because she decided to try and beat the shit out of me," Jake laughed. "I almost put the car in the ditch."

"I will try to get Nikki to calm down," Chance stated.

"Good luck with that," Jake laughed. Chance walked to the car. Nikki was in the back seat screaming in outrage.

"Get back here, you mother fucker. Get me fuck out of the car!" Nikki screamed, throwing her body against the seat.

Nikki couldn't move her arms because the bastard tied a rope around her wrists and body, so her upper torso was mobile. The son of bitch pulled the car off the side of the road after she tried to strangle him from behind. The man tied her up so Nikki couldn't get her arms loose. He had no idea that she found a utility knife under the seat.

Nikki quickly maneuvered the knife with her feet putting it on the seat next to her. She silently watched him drive while scooting over the seat, turning her body so she could pick up the knife. The man pulled the car up to a warehouse where an airplane sat with two other men watching the car approach. Nikki quickly used her hands to feel and opened the knife. She cut the rope off her wrists and then quickly unwrapped the rope from her body.

Nikki decided she was going to fight with everything inside of her. She quickly looked for something to use as a weapon. Nikki found a tire iron and gun under the seat. The gun was empty, but she could still use it if need be. Nikki decided the tire iron would work the best and gripped it firmly in her hand as she watched one of the dark hairy men walking towards the car.

Chance slowly approached the car. He saw Nikki in the back seat, watching him approach the car. Chance stood by the door. He took a deep breath.

"Nikki, it is Chance. I am going to open the door, baby," Chance said, looking inside the car.

"Fuck you, fucking liar," Nikki yelled.

"Nikki, please. I am not lying to you. It is Chance."

"Don't you dare touch me, you piece of fucking shit. I will fucking kill you," Nikki screamed, holding tightly to the tire iron, waiting to strike.

Chance slowly opened the door. Nikki flew out at him, kicking and screaming. According to Jake, Chance was confused for a second because Nikki was supposed to be tied up. Chance saw something shiny in her hands before it connected with him. Nikki swung the tire iron with everything she had, hitting Chance in the hip. Chance almost fell to the ground.

"Fuck!" Chance yelled.

Nikki came out of the car swinging the bar at him again. Chance backed up, watching her swing the bar; she missed him by a few minutes but kept coming at him, swinging the tire iron wildly.

"Nikki put that fucking bar down!" Chance yelled.

"Fuck you, asshole!" Nikki screamed, coming at him again. Nikki managed to hit him in the arm.

"Son of bitch, Nikki, drop the fucking bar!" Chance yelled, trying to grab the bar out of her hand.

"Fuck off!" Nikki screamed, swinging the bar at him.

Chance and Nikki circled each other. Nikki felt a light sheen of sweat cover her body, and her breathing was heavy from swinging the bar with all her might.

"Nikki, calm down. Please, baby, it is Chance. I came to take you home. I have a disguise on, but it is me, baby," Chance stated.

"You fucking liar," Nikki screamed, still swinging the bar at him.

"Nikki, remember the last time we were together. We had a great time in my hot, drinking wine and fooling around. Baby, it is Chance. I have a disguise on. That was the only way to get to you. Please listen to me, baby," Chance said in a calming voice.

Nikki stopped swinging the bar. She stood still, looking at him, scared to believe it was Chance. She kept a hold of the bar. Nikki didn't trust him yet.

"Why am I here?" Nikki asked.

"You were delivering a shipment and got caught in a storm. One of the boxes broke open. You then found cocaine and disposed of it. Which lead you to where you are now." Chance stated. Tears started rolling down Nikki's cheeks.

"Oh my god, Chance, it is really you?" Nikki cried.

"Yeah, baby, it is. I told you I was coming for you," Chance replied.

Nikki dropped the bar and ran to Chance. He caught her in his arms. Nikki was crying hard and kissing his neck. Chance held on to her tightly.

"God, baby, I am sorry this happened to you," Chance whispered, stroking her back.

"I thought I was going to end up dead," Nikki cried.

"I know, baby, so did I." Chance held her while she cried. Her whole body was trembling.

"Shush baby, I got you now. I am taking us home," Chance whispered. Nikki shuttered at his words. She finally stopped crying. Nikki raised her head, looked into his eyes, and gave him a weak smile.

"I am glad you found me," Nikki said.

"You have Colin to thank and Jake to thank. They did all the work."

"How?"

"I will tell you everything on the flight home. We need to leave now." Chance stated firmly. Nikki nodded her head in agreement. Chance led her to the plane with his arm wrapped around her waist. They stopped in front of Colin and Jake. Nikki looked at both of them.

"Thank you so much," Nikki said with tears rolling down her cheeks in gratitude. Jake and Colin nodded their heads.

"Chance will fly you out of here. He will explain everything to you that you need to know. Take care, Nikki; chance, remember what we discussed. I will be in touch," Colin said.

"Colin, be careful," Chance replied.

"Always," Colin replied, smiling and squeezing Chance's shoulder. Colin and Jake started walking to the car. Chance and Nikki climbed inside the plane.

Chance sat down in the cock pit and started the plane, radioing the tower to let them know he was ready to take off. Nikki sat down in the co-pilot seat next to him. Nikki started to fidget and wring her hands together. She kept glancing out the window nervously. Chance received the okay to taxi down the runway.

"Nikki, everything is okay. I am taking you home, baby. Please relax," Chance said softly, looking over at her. He throttled up the plane and taxied down the runway. The plane was airborne. Chance heard Nikki let out the deep breath she had been holding.

"Relax, we are homebound now."

"I can't wait to see the real you. I don't like your disguise."

"So you don't like me all dark and handsome?"

"Yes, you are still gorgeous, but I like the real you better."

"I was sort of glad you didn't recognize me but also a little disappointed."

"Juan had me so drugged up. I would have thought I was hallucinating seeing you."

"Nikki, you will go through withdrawal from not having the coke. Roger said Juan keep you on coke for the last week and a half."

"Oh my god! I didn't know it was that long. I thought it had been only a couple of days. Wait, how do you know Roger?" Nikki asked, confused. Chance glanced at her deciding how much to tell her.

"Jake, the man who bought you, and my brother Colin knew Roger. Roger told Jake that Juan had him hooked on the coke."

"Oh god, that is why I feel like my skin is crawling, and I have a bad headache." Nikki looked down, watching her hands begin to shake.

"We will get you some help for the withdrawal as soon as we get home."

"Chance, I am afraid that Hector will come after me."

"Nikki, you know you can't go to your home, right?" Chance said softly. Nikki looked at him with surprise. Nikki realized she couldn't go back to her normal life. The Stamos brothers would know and come to kill her.

"Oh fuck! What am I going to do?" Nikki cried out in distress.

"Babe relaxes; we will figure it all out."

"Relax! I can't relax. Those fuckers have destroyed my life. I have nothing, no home, and no business. I let the fucking greed of money cloud my fucking judgment, and now it destroyed me," Nikki cried.

"Nikki, please take a deep breath," Chance glanced over at concerned. He reached over, covering her hand with his squeezing. Chance could see Nikki was visibly shaking. She rocked her body back and forth in her seat, crying.

"What am I going to do?" Nikki cried.

"Honey, you will figure it out. Just close your eyes and try to relax. You are mentally exhausted. You need to rest your mind and body for a little bit." Chance said softly. Nikki looked over at him and nodded in agreement. She gave him a weak smile, took a deep breath, and exhaled. Nikki laid her head back on the seat. It only took a few minutes, and Nikki was fast asleep.

Chance glanced over at her. He knew Nikki was exhausted. Chance was relieved that she had fallen asleep. Hopefully, Nikki would sleep the rest of the six hours at home.

Chance wondered if Colin called Carter. He didn't understand why Colin had to stay there. He would find out more from Carter.

Chance felt sick with worry for Nikki. He figured Nikki would be in a lot of distress soon from being without cocaine.

Chance heard going through withdrawal was horrible. Nikki was sleeping soundly right now. She did moan out loud a few times. Nikki was still dressed in the sheer dressing gown from the auction. Chance could see her breasts and the outline of her gorgeous toned body. He hoped Colin would remember to tell Carter to meet them at the airport and to bring Nikki some different clothes.

Nikki had slept for three hours. She woke up feeling sick and broke out in a cold sweat. Her body began shaking from head to toe uncontrollably.

"Chance, I don't feel so well," Nikki said, wrapping her arms around her stomach.

"What's the matter, honey?" Chance asked, concerned, glancing over at her. He could see Nikki was pale and visibly shaking.

"I think I am going to be sick," Nikki moaned. Nikki quickly undid the seat belt and climbed out of the cockpit. She moves quickly to the back of the plane, finding a trash can. Nikki vomited several times into the trash can. Her body was shaking uncontrollably, and a light sheen of sweat covered her. Nikki fell to the floor. Her body started to go into a seizure.

"Nikki, are you all right?" Chance yelled. He got no answer. "Nikki, answer me." Still no response from the back of the plane.

Chance put the plane on autopilot. He unsnapped the seat belt and climbed out of the pilot seat. Chance walked to the back of the plane. He saw Nikki on the floor. Her body was flopping around.

"Fuck!" Chance yelled, kneeling down beside her. Nikki was having a seizure. Her eyes were rolled up, and her mouth had foam in the corners.

"I am here, baby," Chance whispered in a worried voice. Chance had to let the seizure ride out of her system. He ensured Nikki didn't hurt herself as her body trembled and flapped around. Nikki's body finally relaxed. Her eyes finally focused then tears rolled down her cheeks.

"Chance, my whole body hurts," Nikki cried.

"I know, baby. You just had a seizure from withdrawal."

"Oh god!" Nikki moaned, then grabbed the trash can again, gagging. Her stomach clenched hard. She heaved and heaved, but there was nothing inside of her. She couldn't believe the pain in her stomach. It was horrible like someone was trying to literally rip it out.

Nikki doubled over in pain. Her body was covered in sweat and shaking badly. Every part of her body hurt.

"Chance, I feel like I am being ripped apart," Nikki cried. Chance rubbed her back.

"I will get you a bottle of water. You need to drink a lot of water to flush that fucking shit out of your system."

Chance stood up and walked to the small fridge, grabbing a water bottle. Chance handed her the bottle of water. She drank about half of the bottle and then vomited it back up.

"Nikki, you must drink a little at a time, honey. Do you remember the last time you ate anything?" Chance asked. Nikki shook her head.

"I have no idea. My head hurts; it feels like it will explode everywhere," Nikki screamed, grabbing her head and crying.

Chance sat on the floor next to her and pulled her onto his lap. He cradled Nikki as she cried out. Her body shook with the need for the drug she didn't have.

"Shush, baby, you will get through this. You are one strong woman. This will not beat you, Nikki."

After a few minutes of him cuddling her, Nikki struggled out of his hold. She stood up and began to pace back and forth in quick circles.

"Oh god! I need a fix bad, Chance. I feel like I am going to crawl out of my skin," Nikki said, pulling her hair and then rubbing her arms up and down frantically.

"Nikki, we are almost home. We have just a few more hours," Chance said, unsure what to do for her.

"Fuckers! I don't have a home. Those fuckers took my home from me! I hate those mother fuckers!" Nikki screamed in frustration.

Chance had to go check on the autopilot. He went back to the cockpit to check on the autopilot. When he turned to go back to Nikki, she was standing right behind him.

"Why the fuck did you fucking rescue me! You should have left me there to die! Now, I fucking have nothing left, you fucking asshole!" Nikki yelled and poked Chance in the chest.

"Leave you there to be someone's sex slave! Is that what you wanted, Nikki?" Chance stated.

"Fuck you! I am going to have to live on the fucking streets now anyway! I might as well sell my fucking self!" Nikki screamed. Chance shook his head in frustration. He knew Nikki was having withdrawal and was talking nonsense, but it still pissed him off.

"My life was fine until you fucking came along. This is your entire fucking fault. You and your do-goody brothers fucking jinxing me. I wish I never fucking met you, Chance Black!" Nikki screamed and poked him in the chest again.

"Stop it, Nikki, you are talking nonsense," Chance replied.

"Nonsense, you fucking jerk!" Nikki screamed, then pulled her arm back. She slapped Chance hard across the face. Chance was surprised by the attack. He just stood there. His face stung where she had slapped him.

"I fucking hate you, Chance Black!" Nikki screamed and tried to slap him again, but this time, Chance grabbed her hand before it made contact.

Chance started at her with hurt in his eyes. He knew Nikki didn't mean what she was screaming, but hearing her yell it at him still hurt. Nikki's eyes rolled up in her head, and her body dropped to the floor like a sack of potatoes. Her whole body trembled and jerked with the second seizure. Chance ran his hand over the face caressing.

"Relax, Nikki, I am here, baby," Chance whispered. Nikki groaned as her body finally relaxed.

"That's it, baby, relax," Chance whispered.

Finally, the seizure let loose, and her body began to relax. Nikki was breathing heavily. Tears slid from her eyes down her face. She rolled onto her side. Nikki curled into a ball, moaning in pain as her stomach clenched in need. Nikki laid with her back to Chance. Chance tried to comfort her, but she didn't want him to touch her. Nikki slapped his hands away from her. Chance touched her back to caress, but she moved away from him.

Chance tried stroking her head, but she again moved away. Chance finally stood up.

"Okay, I will leave you alone, Nikki," Chance whispered, then walked towards the cockpit.

Nikki wanted to be left alone in her misery. She didn't want Chance to comfort her after the mean things she had just said to him. Nikki felt guilty for her words. She didn't mean them but had felt furious and wanted to hurt someone else like she was hurting.

Nikki had seen the pain in his eyes when she started screaming at him but couldn't help it. She figured she would apologize later, but she was in pain right now. Every part of her body hurt. Chance was the only one here for her to take her anger out on.

Nikki felt like she was being torn into. She laid still and soon slid into a sleep from exhaustion. After half an hour, Chance returned to check on Nikki, finding her still lying on the floor. Chance bent down and realized Nikki was asleep. He didn't want to disturb her.

Chance found a blanket and put it on her as Nikki lay on the floor in a curled ball. Chance sighed in relief that she was sleeping and walked back to the cockpit. He sat down and checked the instrument panel. Everything up front was fine. In a couple of hours, they would land.

Chance flew into Dallas. The tower gave him the clearance to land. He had a smooth landing and taxied the plant to the warehouse. He spotted Carter standing beside his black Escalade. Chance parked the plane in the warehouse. Once the plane was secure, he returned to where Nikki lay on the floor. Nikki was sitting up, holding her head in her hands.

"Nikki, we just landed. Carter is here. He brought you some different clothes," Chance stated. Nikki nodded and groaned.

"I will be right back," Chance said, opening the exit door.

Carter already had a set of stairs against the door. Chance walked down the stairs towards Carter. Carter had a surprised look on his face as Chance walked towards him.

"Holy shit! Is that you, Chance?" Carter asked. Chance had forgotten he still had his disguise on.

"Yeah, sorry. I forgot to tell you I would be in disguise," Chance said, laughing.

"I seriously didn't recognize you at first."

"It was all Colin's doing. Colin's friend definitely knows what to do to change someone's looks. Nikki didn't recognize me either, which was good considering the situation.

"Sometimes you need to be a camellia to get around."

"You guys all had to do secretive jobs. This was my first. Colin knew what he was doing. I couldn't have gotten Nikki back without him. Colin is an entirely different person working a job. I was actually impressed. I am glad Colin came with me."

"Yes, our little brother is excellent at what he does."

"Yes, he is. I am grateful for his training."

"How is Nikki doing?" Carter handed Chance a bag.

"Not good. Nikki is starting to have withdrawals from the cocaine. I'll give these to her and be right back." Chance said. Carter nodded his head. Chance walked back up the stairs and into the plane. Nikki was still sitting on the floor.

"Nikki, here are some clothes for you to put on," Chance said, handing her the bag.

"You don't like what I am wearing?" Nikki asked sarcastically.

"I do, but Carter doesn't need to see you half-naked."

"Why not? I was being sold as a sex slave. At least 50 men saw me naked tonight. Carter might like what to try out the good," Nikki said smartly, untied the ribbon at her waist, then held the sides open to Chance. Chance looked at her and shook his head.

"Carter is a happily married man. So knock the fucking sarcasm off and get dressed," Chance said harshly, tossing the bag to her.

Nikki looked at him, giving him a fake smile. She could tell Chance didn't like her comments. His jaw was clenching in frustration. She grabbed the bag from him.

"I will be outside with Carter when you get dressed. Come on out." Chance stated and walked off the plane.

Nikki got dressed in a pair of sweatpants and a sweatshirt. She throws the sheer gown into the bag. Nikki's hands shook and held onto the bag. She felt tremors run through her body. Nikki felt the light sheen of sweat develop on her skin. She licked her suddenly dry lips needing a fix badly. Nikki had to sit down for a few minutes, rocking back and forth on the chair. Nikki wasn't sure how she would get through the rest of the day, or days for that fact, without the cocaine.

Chance walked down the plane stairs shaking his head in frustration. He knew Nikki was going through withdrawals, which would get harder on her. But she could at least show some appreciation for getting different clothes.

"Everything all right?" Carter asked, concerned, seeing the frown lines on Chance's face.

"Yeah, Nikki is just being sarcastic. I keep trying to remember she is having withdrawal from not having cocaine."

"Nikki is going to go through a couple of hard days and weeks."

"Yeah, I know. Nikki is not happy right now. She blamed me for everything that had happened to her."

"That is because you are the only one around. You need to take Nikki to a drug rehab center right away. The sooner, the better for her and you."

"Yes, I know. I am going to take Nikki to my house first. Then talk to her about getting help."

"Chance, you really need to do it now. Take her to the drug rehab first, then explain how her life will change. Her whole life is going to be turned upside down. "

Nikki walked down the stairs towards them. Chance's sweat pants and sweatshirt were bagging on her, but at least she was fully covered.

"Hello, Carter," Nikki said with a weak smile.

"Glade, you are here, Nikki," Carter said, smiling.

"I am here, but I have nothing left to live for," Nikki replied sarcastically, wrapping her arms underneath her breasts.

"Sure you do. You are alive. That is what matters." Carter stated.

"Yeah, well. I feel like I could die."

"Nikki, it will pass in time. You are a strong woman. You will kick this in no time."

"I hope you are right," Nikki replied softly. Chance noticed Nikki was shaking.

"Nikki, are you cold?" Chance asked softly. Nikki shook her head.

"No, I need a fix badly. I suppose neither of you could hook a girl up with powder?" Nikki asked, hopefully. Carter and Chance shook their heads.

"You both are fucking useless," Nikki murmured.

"Nikki, I am sorry," Chance stated, touching her arm. Nikki pulled her arm away from him.

"No, you're not."

"You are correct, Nikki. I am not sorry I don't have cocaine for you. I am sorry you got yourself into this situation, and the mother fucker Juan Stamos got you hooked on fucking cocaine, but I am not sorry for my brother Colin and his friend Jake for putting their lives on the line to rescue the Stamos brothers. Now stop feeling fucking sorry for yourself and use your anger to fight the addiction, not me." Chance stated firmly. Carter wanted to applaud his brother for putting Nikki in her place.

"I am sorry. I am in a bad way right now, Chance." Nikki said softly.

"I realize that, so let's get it taken care of," Chance said.

Chance helped Nikki climb into the back seat of the truck. Once she was settled in, Chance climbed into the passenger side. Carter climbed into the driver's side and pulled out onto the road.

Nikki sat in the back seat feeling anxious and angry. She was having trouble sitting still. Nikki's legs were trembling. She bounced them up and down quickly, trying to relieve the tension. She twisted her hands together in the lap.

Nikki wanted to lash out at Chance some more. She felt like she could scream bloody murder at the top of her lungs. Nikki felt like she was going to crawl out of her skin. She rubbed her arms up and down rapidly as her legs did the same. Nikki's mouth was dry, and she kept licking her lips, but it was not helping. She wanted to scream out her frustration.

Carter pulled into Chance's driveway and parked. Chance climbed out of the passenger seat and moved to the back, opening the back door.

"Where are we?" Nikki asked, looking at Chance.

"At my house," Chance replied.

"Why?"

"Because we cannot take you to your house."

"This is fucking stupid."

"Nikki, please climb out of Carter's truck so he can go home to his wife."

"At least he has a home to go to," Nikki said sarcastically, climbing out of Carter's truck. Chance tried to help her, but Nikki slapped his hands. Chance turned his attention to Carter.

"I will call you later. Thanks for the ride." Chance said. Carter nodded his head. Chance watched Carter back out of the driveway.

"Come on, let's go inside, Nikki," Chance said softly. Nikki followed Chance to the door. Chance unlocked the door holding it open for Nikki to go inside. He followed Nikki inside his home. Chance left his luggage by the door. Nikki walked into the house and stood in the doorway.

"Are you hungry? I know I am?" Chance asked as he walked towards the kitchen.

"Um. I am not sure." Nikki said, looking around his home.

"Well, I am. I am going to make some breakfast since it is only 10:00am. First, I need to get out of this disguise." Chance stated. Nikki followed Chance into the kitchen.

"Have a seat if you wish," Chance said, pointing to the chairs. "I will be right back."

Chance left the kitchen, heading to the bathroom. He walked into the bathroom and looked into the mirror with a smile.

"Goodbye, Daniel Malcolm," Chance said, pulling off the wig. Next to leave his face was the goatee and mustache. Chance throw everything in the wastebasket. Chance took the brown contacts out of his eyes, tossing them into the trash. He looked into the mirror, glad to see the familiar face looking back at him. The face looking at him had a lot of stress lines right now. Chance sighed and walked out of the bathroom and back into the kitchen.

Chance saw that Nikki was sitting at the counter with her head down. She was twisting her hands nervously in her lap. Nikki didn't even look at him when he entered the kitchen. Chance walked over to the fridge.

"Chance, what am I going to do now?" Nikki asked softly.

"First of all, you need to get help with the drugs Juan gave you. That is the most important thing right now. Everything else can wait until your system is clean of the rotten shit. Once your mind is clear from the drugs, everything else will fall into place."

"I need to get my stuff and money out of my house."

"You can't go home for a while. Hector could be checking your house for any evidence pointing to him. The Stamos will make sure there is nothing to incriminate them."

"Fuck, I have some money stashed at the warehouse in a locker where I keep my plane. The rest is in a safe deposit box."

"Hector paid you in cash?"

"Always, so Hector doesn't have to worry about the evidence against him. I don't have anything. I never recorded the flights I did for him."

"Does Hector know that?"

"Yes, I told him since he was paying in cash. I wouldn't report or record the flights or shipments."

"Hector had it made with you. If you had got caught trafficking drugs, there would have been no evidence connecting Hector to you. You would have taken the fall alone."

"I guess I never thought of it that way. I just really liked the money he paid me. I never realized I was transporting drugs. I probably should say I didn't care. You know the saying, what you don't see will not hurt you. Well, when I did see it, it hurt me."

"It didn't matter if you didn't see or know about it. You would have still gone to prison for trafficking illegal drugs."

"Man, when did I get so messed up? I had my life all figured out when I was in the Air Force. I should have stayed in the Air Force."

"I sometimes feel the same way. But now I have Black Security to keep me busy." Chance put a plate of French toast, scrambled eggs, and ham before her. "Eat. You will need to keep your strength up."

"It does look and smell delicious."

"Dig in and eat." Chance handed her a cup of coffee also. He sat down next to Nikki and started eating. Nikki watched him eat and then took a bit of the food. She didn't realize how hungry she was until she put the food into her mouth.

"I don't remember the last time I eat. This is excellent."

Chance smiled and was glad to see Nikki eating. Nikki probably had not been fed very well in captivity. He was going to ask but figured Nikki probably didn't know since she had been drugged up.

Nikki had just answered his question, saying she couldn't remember the last time she had eaten. They both finished eating in silence. Chance stood up, grabbed the empty plates, and rinsed them in the sink. Nikki sat quietly at the counter while Chance filled the sink with water.

Nikki's stomach started to cramp up a little bit. She tried to rub the cramping away. Her skin broke out in a cold sheen of sweat. Nikki began to feel nauseous.

"Bathroom!" Nikki yelled, holding her hand over her mouth. Chance turned around, seeing Nikki as pale as a ghost.

"Down the hallway," Chance said, pointing to the hallway.

Nikki jumped off the chair and ran down the hallway to find the bathroom. She quickly rushed inside, throwing the toilet seat up, then vomited inside the toilet. Nikki vomited up everything she had just eaten. A cold sweat broke out on her skin. Her heart started racing like it would bust out of her chest. Nikki's stomach clenched in pain. She doubled over and fell onto the floor in pain.

Chance had given her a few minutes of privacy before he decided to check on her. He walked down the hallway to the bathroom. The door was closed. Chance tried to open the door, and it was locked. Chance felt a wave of panic. He knocked on the door.

"Nikki, are you all right?" Chance yelled.

All Nikki could do was moan in pain. She was curled into a ball on the floor next to the toilet. Her body started to shake uncontrollably.

"Oh god!" Nikki moaned in pain, holding her stomach.

"Nikki, please answer me," Chance yelled. There still was no response from Nikki. Chance ran to the kitchen and found a pin to pop the bathroom door lock. He hurried back to the bathroom, put the pin in the lock hole, and popped the lock. When Chance opened the door, Nikki was on the floor, curled in a ball, shaking. Chance rushed over to her side, kneeling down.

"Nikki, can you hear me?" Chance asked, worried. Nikki looked at him and nodded her head.

"I ...hurt...I ...hurt," Nikki sputtered out.

Chance caressed her face and hair. Her forehead and hairline were wet from sweating. Chance stood up and grabbed a washcloth out of the cabinet. He turned on the water and put the washcloth under the cold water getting it wet. He turned the water off and wrung out the washcloth of excess water. Chance knelt beside Nikki again. He wiped her face and neck with the cold washcloth. Nikki began to relax a little bit.

"It will pass, honey. It will pass," Chance murmured, wiping her face.

Nikki lay on the floor shaking. After a few minutes, her stomach stopped clenching in pain. Nikki was still shaking but not as bad. She slowly uncurled her body and then slowly sat up.

"Chance, I am sorry," Nikki whispered.

"You have nothing to be sorry about, Nikki. Juan did this to you. You didn't do this to yourself."

"Technically, I did, so I guess I deserve to suffer for it."

"Nikki, no one deserves to be given drugs against their will or sold like cattle at auction. You were doing a job you thought was legit."

"I know, but I should have treated Hector like all my other clients. But the greed of money got in the way of rational thinking. It was too good to turn away. So now I am paying for the mistake."

"You just need to concentrate on getting through this first. The rest will fall into place. I will help as much as I can."

"Wow, does that mean you care a little bit for me?"

"Yes, I do care, Nikki. I really like you a lot, so I do care."

"Well, that is good to know."

"How about we get off the bathroom floor and sit on the couch. It has to be a little more comfortable than the floor."

"Chance, by the way, your food was delicious. I am sorry I just wasted it." Nikki said sincerely. Chance laughed, helping Nikki up off the floor.

"No worries," Chance laughed. They walked out of the bathroom to the living room, sitting on the couch.

"I guess we better look up drug rehab centers for me. I don't want you to have to take care of me. Besides, it will get worse before it gets better," Nikki said. Chance reached over and squeezed her hand. He got up to get his laptop.

Chance sat back down next to Nikki, opening up his laptop. He put drug rehab centers in the search bar. They found several close by. Chance called one, putting them on speaker so Nikki could hear, and was told the best thing was to get her to them as soon as possible. She would go through some awful episodes in the next few days, worse than what she was already experiencing.

The rehab center had the experience to make it a little easier on the patient. After Chance hung up, he looked at Nikki and smiled.

"So what do you think, Nikki?" Chance asked gently.

"Um... I think we should probably head over there. I am nervous. But I don't want to feel this way anymore."

"You heard them say you won't be able to have visitors for a couple of weeks to a month, depending on how well you do."

"I think it is probably for the best."

"Okay, let's get you over there so you will start to feel like your old self again."

Nikki nodded her head nervously. Chance stood up, holding out his hand to her. Nikki took his hand, standing up from the couch. They walked to the door hand and hand. Chance grabbed his keys then they walked out to his truck. Chance opened the passenger door for Nikki. Nikki climbed inside, closing the door. Chance walked over to the driver's side, climbing inside the truck.

He looked over at Nikki and smiled. Nikki gave him a weak smile. She was nervous and anxious as Chance backed out of the driveway. He reached over, grabbing her hand into his, giving it a reassurance squeeze.

"You got this, Nikki. You are a strong-willed woman and will beat it with flying colors."

"God, I hope you are right, Chance."

"I know I am right. I will check on you every day." Chance promised. The comment made Nikki relax a little bit. Chance pulled into the driveway of Second Chances. Nikki read the name of the rehab center and giggled. Chance climbed out of the truck walking over to the passenger side. He opened the door for Nikki. Nikki climbed out, taking a deep breath and exhaling. She turned to look at Chance.

"Will give me a second chance when I get out of here, Chance Black?" Nikki asked softly as they walked towards the entrance of Second Chances.

"You bet I will," Chance whispered, then kissed her as they entered the building. They walked to the reception area. The woman smiled at them.

"Can I help you?" The woman asked, looking at Chance and then Nikki.

"Um...I need help." Nikki answered.

"Okay, what is the help for?" The woman asked.

"I hooked on cocaine," Nikki replied. The woman nodded her head.

"Okay, let's get you taken care of," the woman stated.

"The sooner, the better, so I can get back to this handsome great man," Nikki stated, smiling.

"I would say he is an incentive for you to get better."

"Yes, he is."

"I will let you say goodbye, then get you registered," The woman said, smiling. Nikki turned her attention to Chance.

"See you soon."

"Yes, you will; that is a promise," Chance smiled.

Nikki nodded her head. Nikki walked away with the nurse. She stopped little ways and turned to look at Chance. She smiled and then blew him a kiss. Chance laughed. Nikki still had her sense of humor. Nikki and the nurse turned down a corner, and Chance couldn't see her anymore. He took a deep breath and then walked back out to his truck.

Chance pulled out of the parking lot and headed to Black Security. He had to find out about Colin. Chance knew Carter would have the answers and wanted to know them. Chance pulled into the parking lot about 15 minutes later. He parked his truck and then climbed, heading to the building. Chance walked into the office. Lillie was sitting at her desk. She looked up with surprise at seeing Chance.

"Chance, what on earth are you doing here?" Lillie asked, concerned.

"I just took Nikki to the Second Chance drug rehab center. I needed to talk to Carter about Colin."

"They will treat Nikki well there. She will get all the help she needs to recover and get clean."

"I hope so. I am just glad Nikki went willingly. She is a very strong woman."

"Yes, she is. Nikki will be okay and back to normal in a few weeks."

"Thanks, Lillie. Now I am going to see your husband." Chance walked to Carter's office. He knocked on the door and went inside. Carter looked up in surprise.

"Hey, Chance. I recognize you now." Carter smiled, leaning back in his chair. Chance smiled.

"I am back to being me again. Have you heard from Colin?"

"Yes, Colin called about a couple of hours ago."

"What is going on, Carter? Why did Colin stay there?"

"Well, you know Jake is the one that brought Nikki for you."

"Yes, Colin informed me while the bidding was going on. Colin didn't have enough money to continue to bid on Nikki. Jake stepped in."

"Well, Colin made a deal with Jake. The deal was, if Jake brought Nikki for you, Colin would stay and help Jake find the Congressman's daughter. Colin is back to doing undercover work."

"So does that mean Colin reenlisted in the Marines again?"

"Well, sort of; Colin is there to help Jake out. You know Colin is posing as a sex slave buyer. Juan contracted him for a business proposal. Colin is unsure what it might involve but will meet with Juan and Joseph tonight. What Colin is doing is very dangerous, but he knows what he is doing. Jake and Colin believe the Stamos brothers are targeting the Congressman's daughters. They are not sure why yet but intend to find out. Congressman Patterson's daughter came missing while you two were in Costa Rica."

"Holy shit, so Jake and Colin think Juan and Joseph are behind her coming up missing?"

"Yes, they do. I am sure it has something to do with politics. Hector Stamos rubs elbows with Congressman Collins and Congressman Patterson. Now both of their daughters came up missing. Neither man is talking. I am sure it has something to do with dirty laundry; it usually does. They are trying to cover something up, and I am sure Hector Stamos is involved somehow."

"Well, you guys have dealt with that kind of shit. I can say I never have. I just flew a helicopter in Afghanistan. I dealt with terrorists in the war zone, not one-on-one like you guys have."

"I am glad you haven't. I have too many battle scars from dealing with them one on one."

"I just hope Colin will be all right. He is a different man while working. Colin is a hard ass and can turn his emotions off completely."

"You have to when you are doing that kind of job. You can't let them break you, or you are dead."

"Is Colin going to keep you informed on what he is doing?"

"Colin will keep me informed as much as he can."

"Well, I guess I will try to get some work done."

"Sounds like a plan. I have a bunch of invoices to put into the system. It will keep me busy for a few hours.

"Better you than me."

"Asshole."

Chance left Carter's office and went to his own. he sat at his desk. He hoped Colin was going to be all right. He also hoped Nikki was doing fine.

Chapter 22

Nikki had been in drug rehab for a month. Chance kept in touch with the staff members to find out Nikki was doing. He was not able to visit her until she had a clean bill. Nikki was excited to finely be able to leave. The Second Chances rehab center called Chance to let him know Nikki was free to go. Chance agreed to pick Nikki up. Nikki was feeling a little nervous but excited to be able to get on with her life again, drug-free.

During therapy, Nikki had a lot of time to think. She had yet to tell Chance her decision. They had not discussed what Nikki was going to do with her life. Nikki finished packing what little she had. There was a soft knock on the door.

"Nikki, it is Chance," Chance stated on the other side of the door.

Nikki smiled, grabbed her bag, and headed for the door. She opened the door with a huge smile.

"Hey baby, I am so ready to blow this joint," Nikki laughed as she approached him. Nikki wrapped her arms around his neck and then gave him a quick peck on the lips.

"I bet you are ready. Well, let's get you out of here." Chance laughed.

They walked hand and hand down the hallway. Nikki stopped at the front desk to get her release papers. She gave all the nurses a hug goodbye. Nikki waved to the nurses as Chance, and she walked out of the front door. Nikki let loose of Chance's hand and then twirled in circles laughing.

"Yes, I am free of drugs and clean," Nikki yelled, laughing, spinning in circles. Chance laughed, watching her.

"I am so fucking proud of you, Nikki," Chance stated sincerely.

"I am proud of myself, too," Nikki said, wrapping her arms around his neck. She planted another kiss on his gorgeous lips. "I missed you, Chance Black."

"I missed you, Nikki Curtis," Chance replied, kissing her back.

"Get me out of this place. I am ready to go," Nikki stated. They walked over to Chance's truck. Chance put Nikki's bag into the back seat. Nikki climbed into the truck putting the seat belt on. She smiled hugely over at Chance.

"So, did you decide what you going to do?" Chance asked curiously.

"Yes, but before we get into all that. I want to go to your house and have wild monkey sex," Nikki laughed.

"Seriously?" Chance asked, surprised, raising his eyebrow. Nikki nodded her head laughing. " Okay, my house it is." Chance chuckled.

"Yes!" Nikki yelled and fist-pumped the air. Chance laughed, shaking his head.

"So, are you excited about being free or having wild monkey sex with me?"

"Both!"

Chance drove to his house. He wasn't sure what Nikki had decided to do. Nikki knew she would have to move out of the state, so Hector didn't see her. Chance really didn't want her to go. He cared a lot about her. They walked into the house. Nikki turned to face him and smiled wickedly at him.

"I want to have some fun first before we talk," Nikki said seductively, moving closer to him. Nikki wrapped her arms around his neck. She bent her head and slid her tongue up his neck. Chance snickered.

"I think you have your mind already made up," Chance groaned as her tongue slid around his ear.

Chance wrapped his arms around her, pulling her gently against him. He slid his hands down her ass and caressed and molded her ass. Nikki let go of his ear with her mouth.

Nikki captured his mouth. She ran her tongue across his bottom lip. Nikki slid her tongue between his lips. Their tongues tangled together in need. She devoured his mouth in need and passion.

Chance slid his hands under her shirt. He caressed her back and then unclasped her bra. Chance moved his hands to her large breasts. He pushed her bra up and out of his way. His hands cupped and molded her breasts.

Nikki wiggled in need against him. Chance pinched her nipples into hard peaks. Nikki pulled her mouth from his. She stepped back a few inches and pulled her shirt and bra off. Nikki threw them on the floor.

Chance bent his head and captured her nipple in his mouth. His tongue swirled around her nipple. His other hand cupped and molded her other breast.

Chance switched his mouth to her other nipple to give it some loving. Nikki held his head to her. Chance slid his hand down to her jeans. He unbuttoned and unzipped her jeans. Nikki let go of his head. She slides her jeans and panties off.

Nikki's hands went to his shirt, grabbing the hem of his shirt and pulling it up over his head. Chance unbuttoned and unzipped his pants. He slides them down to his knees. Nikki picked Nikki up by her ass. She instantly wrapped her legs around his waist. Their mouths came together, sucking and licking each other. Chance kicked his jeans, pushing them to the side. He walked over to the nearest wall. He pushed her back against the wall.

Nikki slid her hand down and positioned his hard cock at her wet entrance. She pushed down on him until the head of his cock entered her. Chance started to slowly thrust inside her. Nikki held on to him, moaning at the feel of him inside her.

"You feel so good," Nikki moaned.

"So do you, baby," Chance growled out as he thrusts inside her effortlessly. Nikki was nice and sleek with need.

"Faster, Chance," Nikki groaned. Chance picked up his speed. He felt her walls clenching him.

"I feel your need, Nikki," Chance whispered.

"Oh yeah," Nikki panted.

Chance felt her walls clench his cock harder. He started to pull almost out of her and then slammed back inside of her deep.

"Are you going to come for me?" Chance panted.

"Oh god, right there, Chance!" Nikki cried out. Chance slammed inside her a few more times. She clenched him hard as her orgasm hit.

"Chance," Nikki yelled.

Chance felt her come coat his cock. He pumped hard inside her a few more times. Chance's cock jerked and swelled. He exploded inside her.

"Fuck!" Chance growled as he emptied himself inside her.

They both were trembling from their orgasm. Chance rested his head against hers as his breathing slowed back to normal. Nikki unwrapped her legs from around his waist and put them on the floor. She keep her arms wrapped around his neck.

"Damn, that was good," Nikki whispered against his lips. Chance kissed her.

"Damn, I missed you," Chance kissed her lips a few more times.

"Same here, but I think we better get dressed."

"Why?"

"We need to talk now."

Chance snickered, letting go of her. He bent down, grabbed his jeans, slipping them on. He also grabbed his shirt off the floor and pulled it on. Nikki picked up her clothes and headed to the bathroom.

Chance went to the couch and sat down, waiting for Nikki. Nikki came out of the bathroom all dressed. She walked over to the couch and sat down next to him.

"Do we need some wine, or would you rather have a beer or can of coke?"

"Beer sounds good," Nikki replied, smiling.

Chance stood up, walking to the kitchen. He grabbed a couple of beers from the fridge. He headed back to the living room. He handed her a bottle of beer, sitting next to her. They sat quietly, sipping their beer. Nikki glanced over at him.

"Um... I came to a decision while I was in rehab." Nikki said softly. Chance nodded his head for her to continue.

"I rejoined the Air Force. I will be stationed in Alabama. I re-enlisted for the next four years."

"I am glad."

"I figured that was easier than trying to move to another state and start all over. I won't have to worry about Hector and his sons finding me."

"The Air Force definitely will keep you moving around."

"I enjoyed the Air Force. I still need to figure out why I didn't stay in. I think I was afraid to go into a war zone."

"Nikki, everyone in the military doesn't enjoy going into a fighting zone. But we do what we have to. We all signed up to defend our country."

"I guess you are right. But I was afraid of that part of the package."

"We all are, but you just go and do what is expected. So when do you leave?"

"In two days. I have to get some stuff wrapped up first."

"I will miss you, but you made the right decision."

"I will miss you also. This was the only decision that made any sense to me. I feel like I am going home where I belong and what I know."

"That makes sense. When I first got out of the Air Force, I felt lost. Going into business with my brothers made the loss go away. I know I am where I belong."

"I wish this never happened, Chance. We could have a great relationship.

"Yeah, I feel the same way," Chance replied softly, wrapping his arm around her shoulder and pulling her closer to his side.

"I will not ask for a long-distance love affair. That would not be fair to either of us. But I hope we can hook up when I am in town."

"I would like that very much." Chance reached out, putting his hand under their chin, pushing her head up. He captured her lips in a passionate kiss. Their tongues tangled and twisted together, tasting each other. Chance pulled his mouth from hers. Nikki gave him a smile.

"Chance, I can't thank you and Colin enough for rescuing me," Nikki said sincerely.

"It is not necessary."

"Yes, it is. I hate to think what would have happened if you and Colin hadn't."

"You don't have to think about it anymore. You are getting ready for a new life adventure. Embrace it and fly with happiness in your heart."

Nikki laughed at his comment. "You are so right."

"Never look back at the bad just move forward with a happy heart."

"I never knew you were so sentimental."

Chance laughed. They drank the rest of their beer. Chance stood up and walked to the fridge to grab them another beer. He sat back down next to her. They were quiet for a while, just enjoying being with one another.

"Chance, will you make love to me one time before I have to leave?" Nikki asked quietly.

Chance smiled and nodded his head. He stood up, holding his hand out to her. Nikki smiled as he pulled her up from the couch. They walked hand and hand into his bedroom and stood at the edge of the bed.

"You are so beautiful, Nikki," Chance whispered, staring into her beautiful eyes. Nikki smiled.

"So are you, Chance Black," Nikki said. Chance chuckled.

Nikki reached down to the hem of his shirt, pulling it over his head. Chance did the same with her shirt. They tossed the shirts on the floor. Chance reached behind Nikki's back and unsnapped her bra, slowly pulling it away, revealing her large, beautiful breasts.

"God, woman, I love your tits," Chance whispered, staring at her breasts. Nikki laughed. Chance reached out, caressing them. Nikki slid her hand down to the waistband of his jeans. She unbuttoned and unzipped his jeans. She slides her hand inside his jeans underneath the boxers. Nikki grabbed hold of his stiff cock.

"I love your huge cock," Nikki stated, giving his cock a squeeze. Chance moaned. He slipped his hand down to the waistband of her jeans. He unbuttoned and unzipped her jeans, slipping his hand inside, underneath her panties. His hand cupped her pussy, then slipped a finger between her wet folds.

"You are slick for me," Chance whispered, moving his finger back and forth, feeling her wetness on his finger.

"Only for you," Nikki moaned. She let loose of his cock, pushing his jeans and boxers down over his hips. Chance did the same with jeans. They both finished sliding off their jeans, pushing them aside. Now they were standing next to the bed naked.

Chance picked her up and gently laid Nikki on the bed. He lay down next to her. They turned to their sides to face each other. Chance captured her mouth. Their tongues tangled and twisted together with passion.

Their hands caressed each other bodies, both of them memorizing each other. Nikki wrapped her leg around his hip. Chance reached down, positioned his cock at her entrance, and slowly thrust his hips, entering her slick channel. After a few more thrusts of his hips, he was entirely inside her. Chance stayed still for a few seconds as her body adjusted to his size.

Their bodies moved together as one. Chance rolled on his back, so Nikki was on top of him. Nikki lay stretched out on top of him. Nikki stared into his beautiful eyes as she moved her body against his, making love to him. She was in control of the pace. Nikki bent her head down, capturing his mouth. Their tongues mimic their bodies as they move together.

Chance and Nikki moved their bodies more urgently as the need became more intense. Chance rolled again, so Nikki was beneath him. He sank his cock deeper inside her. He moved in and out, setting the pace faster as their orgasms peaked.

"Come with me, Nikki," Chance whispered. Nikki moaned loudly as her orgasm rushed forward.

"Oh, Chance, right there, baby, right there," Nikki moaned. Her walls clenched down on Chance's cock tightly. Chance growled at the feeling of her clamping on to him in need. He began to slam inside at a faster, deeper pace.

"Yes!" Nikki cried out as she went over the edge. Her pussy pulsated around his stiff cock coating it with her cream.

"Fuck!" Chance growled as his balls drew tight, and his cock jerked and swelled inside her. He felt the white-hot spurts of his come shooting inside her. Chance kept the pace up until he emptied himself. He captured her mouth and pumped the last of his seed inside. Their tongues devoured each other in passion. Their bodies moved against each other at a slower pace. They stayed joined for a while after their orgasm had passed.

Chance rolled off her and lay on his back. Nikki turned to her side to snuggle up to him. Her hand automatically caressed his chest.

"Chance, I wish I could stay beside you forever, but I have to get going and pick up some stuff from my house. Or this will get harder for me to leave," Nikki whispered.

"I understand. I wish the same," Chance said, then kissed her forehead. He unwrapped himself from her. They both climbed out of bed, redressed, and walked to the living room. Chance grabbed his truck keys.

"Are you sure about going to your house?" Chance asked.

"I have to. There are a few things I need to get," Nikki said. Chance nodded his head. They walked to the front door and then out to his truck.

Chance opened the passenger side for Nikki, then closed it behind her. Chance walked over to the driver's side climbing up inside the truck. They were silent as he drove to Nikki's apartment.

"What do you think the Stamos did to my apartment?" Nikki asked as Chance parked in front of her apartment building.

"It is probably trashed," Chance answered honestly.

"You are probably right," Nikki said, taking a deep breath before opening the passenger door. They climbed out of the truck.

"You ready for this?" Chance asked, staring at Nikki. Nikki sighed deeply, nodding her head.

"I have not been here since the day I left to take the shipment to the Stamos brothers," Nikki stated. Chance grabbed her hand, squeezing it as they walked to the front door of her apartment. Nikki slid the key into the lock, unlocking the front door. She took another deep breath and then opened the front door.

"Oh my god!" Nikki cried out, seeing her apartment had been totally trashed. Chance and Nikki stepped inside the apartment.

"Jeezus! They didn't leave one thing untouched," Chance stated, looking at all the ripped and destroyed furniture.

"I hate them, son of bitches, with every fiber inside me. I never wished anyone dead, but I hope they fucking die," Nikki stated with tears falling down her cheeks.

"I am so sorry, Nikki, that happened to you."

"You have nothing to be sorry for. This was all my own fault. I just hope I can find my personal stuff in this fucking mess."

As they walked around the apartment, everything had been destroyed. In the bedroom, every article of clothing had been pulled out of dresser drawers and tossed on the floor. All the clothes in Nikki's closet had been pulled off the hangers and thrown on the floor. Everything in the closet had been pulled out, checked, and tossed on the floor. The apartment looked like a tornado had gone through it.

Nikki searched through the mess, finally finding everything she needed. She grabbed a couple of suitcases and put clothes inside. Once they were full, she grabbed trash bags to put the rest in. They worked quickly and silently. Nikki looked around the bedroom, finding the dresser drawer she had been looking for. She reached inside, finding the taped key inside. Nikki was so glad they didn't find the key. It was the key to a safe deposit box she had. It is where there was $300,000.00 in cash. Nikki twirled in a circle holding onto the key. Chance gave her a questionable look.

"It is a key to a safe deposit box I have money in. I would like you to keep a hold of it for me," Nikki said, looking at Chance with a smile.

"Nikki, are you sure?" Chance asked, surprised.

"Yes, I didn't tell you where the box is located. I can't take the chance of losing the key while I am in the service. So, will you take care of this key for me until I return for it?"

"I would be glad to hold on to the key for you because it will mean you must come back to me."

"I promise. I will be back." Nikki said, handing the key to Chance.

"Shouldn't you make a copy of it just encase you change your meaning? Maybe you will find the love of your life in the service."

"I trust that when the time comes, you will give me the key regardless of if I find the love of my life. The same can go for you also."

“I am not looking right now. I only have eyes for you.”

“You are such a charmer. I am sure you will not stay single for long.”

"Maybe and maybe not. Are you ready to get out of here? We should not hang out here too long.

“I hate to leave all my stuff behind.”

"I know, but you are supposed to be here. We don't know if the Stamos brothers are watching your apartment."

"I didn't think about that. Okay, let's go." Nikki looked around her apartment as tears formed in her eyes without falling. She had worked hard for everything she had, and they had destroyed all of it. Nikki swallowed back the scream she wanted to let loose.

"Are you okay, Nikki?" Chance asked, concerned.

"Yes, I have to be," Nikki replied, walking to the door. She took another look saying goodbye to her old life and hello to her new one.

They walked out to Chance's truck. There was a taxi outside waiting for Nikki. They loaded Nikki's stuff in the trunk of the taxi. After they loaded her stuff in the trunk of the taxi, Chance wrapped his arms around her once again, pulling her close to his body. He bent his head down, capturing her lips in a toe-curling, passionate kiss. Chance devoured her mouth, letting her know how he really felt. His heart was breaking at losing this woman. Chance wanted Nikki to remember this kiss and him while she was away. Chance could taste the tears that mingled in the kiss as they rolled down her face. Chance finally let loose of her mouth, staring into her tear-filled eyes. Nikki gave him a weak smile.

"So long sexy man. I will miss you," Nikki said, smiling.

"Nikki, please keep in touch with me," Chance grinned.

Nikki looked at him for a few more minutes, then nodded. She gave him a quick kiss and pulled out of his arms. Nikki walked towards the passenger side of the taxi and opened the door. She could feel Chance watching her. Nikki turned and smiled. She blew him a kiss and climbed into the taxi.

Chance waved to Nikki with a smile. He felt his heart clench with sorrow but knew she would be fine. He would be fine also as time passed.

THANK YOU FOR DOWNLOADING my e-Book. I hope you enjoyed it as much as I enjoyed writing it.

Other Books by the author

Bad Boys Escort Service Series:

Bad Boys Escort Service - Bronner McCray Book 1

Bad Boys Escort Service - Bo McCray Book 2

Bad Boys Escort Service - Sawyer McCray Book3

Bad Boys Escort Service - Grant McCray Book 4

Bad Boys Escort Service - Westin McCray Book 5

Bad Boys Escort Service - Harley McCray Book 6

Black Security Company Series:

Black Security Company - Carter Black Book 1

Black Security Company - Chase Black Book 2

Black Security Company - Chance Black Book3

Black Security Company - Colin Black Book 4 (coming soon)

About the Author

Sally Lovell is from a small town in Michigan. She is an avid reader with no experience or training in writing books. With encouragement from her family, Sally decided to give writing a try. Writing became a part-time passion since she is still working a full-time job. She has never felt more exhilarated or more alive than losing herself in writing.

www.ingramcontent.com/pod-product-compliance
Lightning Source LLC
Chambersburg PA
CBHW051932190825
31364CB00030B/119
* 9 7 9 8 2 2 7 3 9 8 6 9 7 *